Dear Mystery Lover,

It is with great pride an̲[d̲ ̲ ̲ ̲ ̲ ̲ ̲ ̲ ̲ ̲]to bring
you St. Martin's DEAD L[   ]
The DEAD LETTER p[   ]
Represent all of the mys[   ]
best writers in each. If you're a fan of a specific kind of
mystery, we've got the books to feed your habit. And,
if you're looking for something new, we've got that,
too.

Start your DEAD LETTER library with *The Ballad of
Rocky Ruiz* by Manuel Ramos, a nominee for an Edgar
Award and a national bestseller! This vibrant and lyri-
cal debut novel introduces mystery readers to Denver
attorney Luis Montez and to the rich, fascinating
Chicano culture. **If you are a fan of Walter Mosley's
Easy Rawlins novels or are looking for a fresh char-
acter-driven series, give Manuel Ramos a try.** Like
reviewers nationwide, you'll take Luis Montez into
your heart and be rewarded with "a vivid glimpse of
a culture often overlooked by the genre."* Manuel
Ramos is one of a core of St. Martin's DEAD LETTER
continuing authors and is committed to delivering
more mysteries in the months and years to come.

Keep your eye out for DEAD LETTER—and build
yourself a library of paperback mysteries to die for.

Yours in crime,

Shawn Coyne
Editor
St. Martin's DEAD LETTER Paperback Mysteries

El Mundo Latino

THE BALLAD OF
ROCKY RUIZ

MANUEL RAMOS

ST. MARTIN'S PAPERBACKS

For Flo

THE BALLAD OF ROCKY RUIZ

Library of Congress Catalog Card Number: 93-1109

ISBN: 0-312-95569-3

Printed in the United States of America

St. Martin's Press hardcover edition/July 1993
St. Martin's Paperbacks edition/May 1995

10 9 8 7 6 5 4 3 2 1

PART ONE

◆

*Ojitos bonitos
Que me estan acabando
Ojitos bonitos
Que me estan matando*
"Ay Ojitos"

I don't recall all the subtleties and particulars and some of the events are screwed up in my head—out of sequence, out of synch. Hell, there were too many late nights and fuzzy mornings, and even back then I had a hard time keeping it straight. Life had this rough texture, like Velcro on a screen door. But there is one detail that stands out in my mind as clearly as if I was staring at her this minute, across the room, waiting for her to finish taking off her clothes. Those eyes—the round, moist, glowing brown eyes that will haunt me as sure as *la llorona* prowls dark alleys looking for bad children; eyes that will stay with me until Chicanos reclaim their lost land of Aztlán—forever. There are days when I look over my shoulder and I catch them watching me, driving me up the wall, chilling my skin, making me forget every other woman I knew or met or loved. I know those eyes.

And the blood. I remember the blood. . . .

1

Toby Arriega's jury came back in about forty-five minutes—guilty on enough counts to send him away for at least another eight years, maybe a little more if the judge hammered him with aggravations.

The trial had exhausted me. I was too old for this—taking on work simply because it walked in the door, busting my butt trying to find a witness to back up Arriega's alibi, poring over police reports, talking to the names listed by the DA, calling Toby's brothers and sisters for help, piecing together a defense out of nothing, and getting paid just enough to keep me on the hook until the trial was over. Then the damn jury took less than an hour to decide my effort was worthless.

It was a tough case from the beginning. I didn't particularly care for my client or his relatives. They were a hoodlum bunch from the Westside and they knew more about the criminal-justice system than most judges. They had no qualms about cussing out their lawyer in the courthouse hallway.

I suggested to Toby that he cop out to one of the assault charges, but the old con would not go for it. He was already a two-time loser—what the hell did he care? He knocked over the convenience store, of course. What I couldn't understand was why he beat up the clerks and trashed out the place. Toby denied the rough stuff and said wrecking the joint was the work of a kid, maybe one of the clerks, or another stickup man, angry that Toby beat him to the punch—in any case, it wasn't Arriega. But I couldn't prove that. The clerks fingered Toby, said he locked them up in the back room and pistol-whipped them before he rampaged through the aisles of dog food, loaves of bread, and comic books. And Detective Philip Coangelo finished the job with a very crisp and formal recitation of the incriminating remarks Toby had made when they busted down his door and dragged him away to the city jail.

I ended up in the Dark Knight Lounge, hunched over bourbon and beer, fed up with my scraggly-assed existence as a borderline lawyer who represented guys who should have gone to the public defender or housewives who finally had had it with their fat and usually unemployed husbands. Yes, I was feeling sorry for myself, almost as sorry as Toby would feel when they shackled him in the van for the long, quiet ride to Cañon City and the state pen. At least he knew what he would be doing, and where he would be doing it, for the next several years. I didn't have a clue.

I finished my shot and ordered another, nursing the beer. My gut burned with the liquor's acid. My bones, from eye sockets to ankles, were sore. You'd think Toby had worked me over after the verdict came in. It was only my forty-one-year-old body letting me know, in the cute way it had, that I drank too much, ate all the wrong foods, represented too many of society's dregs, and let the little tensions of life overwhelm me. I stared into the bottom of the empty shot glass, looking for a sign, a hint, anything that might lead me into tomorrow with more than a hangover and an empty wallet.

"You look lousy, Luis. Ain't no big thing, man. It couldn't be that bad." Tino Pacheco wasn't exactly what I had in mind. He was an old friend—damn, who wasn't?—but I had a hard time handling more than a few minutes with him. Unfortunately, Tino would hook into a person for days—months—and his edgy, tough-guy act eventually rubbed off on whoever was with him. Tino had this influence on people. He had a way to make a person talk and act crazy.

Our hands met in a halfhearted attempt at the Chicano handshake, but we didn't quite remember all the intricacies. "Tino. Long time. What's up?"

I put up with Tino because of the old days. When we were young, Tino and I had ended up crawling on the floor more than a few times, usually after a dirty, ugly fight in a bar where the white kids were too sensitive for Tino's insults or the Chicano brothers decided they had had their fill of him.

He had a gleam in his eyes, like mica dust, and he was either higher than a kite or in love. I was drunk enough to be amused. He pushed the girl in my direction, and I knew that Tino's problem was not

4

drugs, not right then. He hung on to a Chicana many years younger than either of us. I checked her out, not expecting much, and I was pleasantly surprised. In the shadowy smoke- and alcohol-induced glaze of the bar, I saw that Tino finally had done something right.

Long black hair framed a thin, seductive neck. Her slender body snuggled against Tino with the right bit of casualness to whet my curiosity.

"Luis, old buddy, I want you to meet Teresa Fuentes. She just graduated from law school, man. A lawyer like you. This is the guy I was telling you about, baby, Luis Montez. Attorney at law and old-time revolutionary pal of mine."

I looked at her face and, you know how it is, there are times when the people, atmosphere, and emotions all come together at the right instant and you swear that life really is fine, after all. The four black musicians on the small, barely lighted stage kicked off their last set with a moody, bluesy jazz harmony that set exactly the right tone. The bourbon cruised my system, mellowing out the rough parts and tricking me into thinking that the city was the only way to go. And I stared into the most beautiful pair of eyes I had seen in years of chasing every manner and style of woman, tearing apart two marriages and who knows how many affairs, living through broken hearts and breaking a few, too. But those eyes turned me into a twenty-one-year-old loco, a dude on the prowl, and the world again was inhabited by beautiful, sensual women. The most beautiful, the most sensual was right there in front of me, rubbing her thigh against macho Tino, to be sure, but now she had met me, and, if Tino was *pendejo* enough to steer her my way, well, *ese, así es la vida,* man.

She offered her dark manicured hand and I took it, compared its color to mine—almost a perfect match—rubbed it, and held it for a few seconds more than was appropriate. She smiled at me and about ten years of crust fell off my skin. "Very nice to meet you, Mr. Montez. I've heard a lot about you." I assumed from Tino, which meant I already could be trash in her eyes.

"Luis will do, Teresa. And don't believe anything Pacheco tells you unless he can produce two witnesses, unrelated." Tino socked me in the arm—"Hey, bud, don't give Teresa the wrong idea"—and a puzzled, worried look creased her forehead. I wanted to touch her face, to assure her that the thing between Tino and me wasn't serious, that it had started somewhere back in the history of our lives too ancient to remember. I massaged the charley horse in my shoulder left by Tino's punch. The guy always had been a pushy son of a bitch.

The night turned into a hazy, gritty smear of strong drinks, loud music, and smoky bars. We bounced around from one joint to another, Teresa drinking one for the three Tino and I guzzled. She was quiet, aloof, and I appreciated the way she surrounded herself with mystery. I tried to stay cool, but I was lost in the booze and every ten minutes or so I caught myself wanting to grab her and kiss her and rush her away to my place.

I couldn't ditch Tino, and the longer the night

lasted, the more belligerent and hostile he became. A half dozen times I had to pull him away from some guy he was going to bust in the mouth or from the victim of one of his unprovoked verbal assaults who was ready to clobber him with a beer bottle. It was obvious he was trying to impress Teresa, but all she gave him was an occasional hug or a little kiss on the cheek and plenty of exasperated sighs. I guess it was enough for him.

Lolly's Taco Shack on West Thirty-Second Avenue has the best jukebox in town—James Brown and Los Gamblers, Al Green and Freddy Fender. At three in the morning, it's usually crowded with Mexicans whooping it up from the dance at the GI Forum hall, suburbanites tasting the edge, and professionals celebrating the fact that everything has gone their way. Teresa and I ended up at Lolly's to put a cap on the night with something other than alcohol. We munched away at menudo, enchiladas, and green chile, listening to a background of kitchen noises and the excited babble of culturally deprived white folks soaking up the color and smells of Denver's Little Mexico.

I tried small talk, but my concentration was shot. Those eyes. I would start to say something and then realize I had been staring at her in silence, taken in by the flashes of color and midnight deep in her eyes, and finally, awkwardly, I would look away or say something stupid.

I figured it was safe to ask about Tino, since he had passed out in the backseat of my car. "How long have you known Pacheco? He doesn't seem to be the type that would be in your circle." The cloud that passed over her face told me I had again turned to stupidity when I had nothing else to say.

"Exactly what is my circle?" Something about my halfhearted attempt to insinuate she lived in a separate, more refined world upset her.

"Okay, okay. How about a simple how did you meet Tino?"

She shrugged, took her time about answering. "He's my landlord, if you can believe that. After the job offer from Graves, Snider and Trellis, I asked around about an apartment, a quiet place to study for the bar exam. When I finished school, I moved up here quick, without much. Someone at the office told me about the Corsican Plaza. Tino's asked me out every week since I've been there, but I was so into the bar, I didn't do anything else for two months. That's over now and I needed to unwind . . . so I took him up on his offer. And here we are." She smiled like a kid who had found a shiny new quarter in the sofa.

Before I lost myself again, I tried talking. "Tino's a little intense, sometimes. I've known him for a long time. He's basically all right. Loyal. Does the best job he can." I wanted to tell her old movement stories, brag about our days as Chicano radicals fighting cops and university deans. I let it go. The old days are harder and harder for me to drag up, especially with a young sweetheart scarcely old enough to remember the big names like Cesar Chavez and Corky Gonzales, let alone care about the grunts of the revolution.

"Sure. I don't have a problem with Tino. He reminds me of my brothers in Brownsville. Talks and struts just like them. A Chicano." That explained that.

She must have been at the top of her class. Had to be close to coax a rise out of the old guys at Graves, Snider and Trellis. The offer was most likely contingent on her passing the bar. She didn't seemed fazed by that. She really was relaxed, almost mellow, and I was knocked out by her attitude. After I took the bar exam, it was a month before I could relax, before I quit rehashing the questions and rewriting the answers in my head, convinced I had blown it. And I did not have the pressure of the best job I had ever been offered riding on the results. I was headed for the legal-aid office and the poor and underprivileged—if I could pass the damn bar. Teresa had already forgotten about the exam.

She would be the first minority woman in the firm, so a certain amount of stress would come with the package. Little things like advising the most racist client one of the unhappy partners could steer her way, or fighting off the heavy-handed sexual maneuvers of her colleagues. But if she showed any ability at all, she'd have it made for the rest of her professional career, provided she didn't mind representing insurance companies and corporate employers and counseling rich codgers about taxes and estates. Several years before, I would have railed at her about selling out, but I didn't have that in me anymore and, as far as I was concerned, she was far too beautiful to argue about political questions that had been debated again and again before she was born or when she was a kid.

"Is your family still in Texas?"

"My mother and one of my brothers are down there. Everybody else has spread out around the country."

"You'll like Denver, Teresa. It's a beautiful city, plenty going on these days. Not much like Texas, though, particularly Brownsville."

I bet myself that she was a good daughter of a traditional Chicano family. Fluent in Spanish—knew about *vatos* and cruising and the Chicano male role playing that her brothers must have shown off whenever they had a chance. A woman I could fall for, forget the eyes.

With some women, you think you know exactly what is going on in their heads; you see it in their faces, the way they wrinkle their foreheads or frown at the corners of their mouths, though often you cannot do anything about what you think you know. Surprise, or joy, or the hurt is right there and it helps clumsy slobs like me deal with them. We struggle to overcome the disadvantage we have whenever we are in the company of women who turn our blood to frozen honey.

Teresa offered no such help. I had not learned the kinds of things I wanted to know about her and she gave up nothing about herself unless I asked. She would be good in court or across the conference table. Opposing counsel would pay trying to figure her out before she lowered the boom. I promised myself to avoid that situation.

The eyes—shining in the restaurant's bright white lights, creating lewd and wonderful visions in my imagination about what the two of us could do with each other. They flared up again at the mention of her hometown. I dipped a piece of tortilla in my menudo and pretended to eat.

"Have you been down there, Luis?"

"Years ago. When I was in college. I had a friend from San Benito. He took me through Texas when we were out on the road. A little Chicano roots trip to Mexico and other points south. Long time ago. Maybe you know his family. His name was Ruben Ruiz. We called him Rocky. You know anybody named Ruiz?"

For the first time that night, she missed a beat. She tried to shovel food in her mouth and answer at the same time, and it didn't work. Her spoon rattled on her plate. The beers were finally catching up.

"No. Not from down home. I don't know any Ruiz. But you're absolutely right. Denver is nothing like Brownsville." She reached across the table and grabbed my hand. "I should go home, Luis. I think I've had it, probably overdid it my first night out since I've been locked up with my bar outlines and law books. And we have to take Tino home."

I held on to her hand. "Right. Good old Tino. We can drop him at his favorite corner. He's used to sleeping it off in the gutter."

Twenty-five minutes later, as I half-carried, half-dragged him into her apartment and then plopped him on her couch, I seriously wondered why we hadn't thrown him in the street. Then I reminded myself that we were buddies, *carnales*, revolutionary comrades, and it would not do to toss him away, no matter how much of an asshole he was, no matter how much I wanted to tell Teresa that we needed to learn more about each other and why didn't I spend the night and show her how sweet an older Chicano with about ten drinks over his limit can be, given the opportunity.

"You sure he'll be okay here? I can take him to my place, let him sleep it off on my back porch. You hardly know this guy."

She laughed as she threw a blanket over the snoring lump. "Quit worrying. He's my landlord. I see him every day. His apartment is one floor under mine. If we knew what he did with his key, we could take him to his place. It doesn't make sense for you to cart him around town so you can bring him back here in the morning. It'll be all right. I can take care of Tino." I left knowing damn well that she could and thinking that Tino better not try anything with her once he came out of his stupor. Something about the strength of Texas women had always brought out my admiration. Or was it the eyes?

2

I spent the next day recovering in my usual foggy, wrung-out fashion. My headache stayed until the late afternoon and I never did swing into the work I had put off because of the Arriega trial. I was tired, mentally and physically. I hadn't yet learned that I could not bounce back from a late-night spree as quickly as I used to when I was twenty years younger.

I caught myself tripping off on the little things about women that stick with me and make no sense at all and often change with different women: her eyes, naturally; the delicate skin around her mouth that wrinkled when she laughed; the way her hand rested on mine in the restaurant.

Tino was a problem. A minor one to be sure, and I wasn't exactly clear about what bothered me. I knew the Corsican Plaza. I had rented an apartment there once when I needed to chill out, and Tino gave me a break. It was difficult for me to believe that somebody at the most prestigious law firm in town had recommended the place. Teresa had not been specific about who made the recommendation. Secretaries, paralegals, and office runners might stay at the Corsican but certainly not lawyers, unless they were drying out after a lengthy binge brought on by a particularly difficult divorce. As far as I knew, I was the only tenant in the Corsican's history who fit that description.

And no way was that place quiet. I did not believe she really studied there, certainly not on Friday nights when the secretaries, paralegals, and office runners started one of their weekend parties to celebrate the death of another tough week in the grimy heart of the city. Whatever, it must have worked for Teresa.

I convinced myself that I could look back on the evening with some perspective, and I had to admit that whatever happened between us, no bells rang, no fireworks exploded over our heads, and we assuredly had not set the night on fire with our lovemaking. The night ended, after all, with Tino sleeping over. By the end of the day, as my hangover mercifully released its hold, I resigned myself to recognizing the limits of our relationship, as embryonic as it was. I threw into the mix my calculations about the difference in our ages.

I'm not anybody's wide-eyed yokel, so the fact that I had seventeen years on her didn't necessarily rule out anything between us. It only made an affair more difficult. She fit neatly into the midlife crisis I was determined to have, and she could absolutely satisfy the sexual fantasies I had created about younger women. What it came down to included

14

long conversations in the middle of the night, complicated explanations because of a missed date or a forgotten promise—entanglements. My infatuation with those eyes could lead to joy, embarrassment, pain. My head suddenly hurt again and it was more than a hangover. The years congealed at the small of my back like a tumor resting on my spine.

I decided to leave the office a little early. On the way out, I bumped into Janice Kendall, one of the attorneys who shared the building and the answering service. She was another ex-legal-aid lawyer, quiet and businesslike in all of her affairs, professional and personal.

"Leaving already, Louie? Must have been a late night."

She knew me too well. We had worked in the same neighborhood office for two years. Amazing what cramped, ugly surroundings and a hectic pace can do for one's interoffice relationships. Hate or love, no in-between. Janice and I at least talked to each other.

"I need a break, Jan. The trial, you know how it is. I can do some things at the house." I lifted my briefcase and waved it at her as if that proved I wasn't about to goof off. Why carry the damn thing if I wasn't going to do some work?

"You bet, Louie. Take it easy." And she vanished into her own office. She was busier than I, well known, a former president of the Women's Bar Association. It didn't hurt my business to have a little professional respect hanging around, particularly if the professional carried herself well in a skirt and a pair of high heels.

15

I called her Shark, not to her face, not to anyone else. She quietly and in cold blood prepared her cases in finest detail. She feasted on the remains of her adversaries, often before they realized they had been wounded. Her court presence was sleek and streamlined—to the point, emphasizing what she needed to win, bringing out the contradictions, mistakes, and oversights in her opponent's case, piling on the favorable evidence from unusual sources until the judge or jury had no choice but to give her the decision, if not in the interest of justice then certainly because she had so tipped Lady Justice's scales by the accumulation of her evidence and arguments that there was no decision to be made. Janice Kendall also was one of the nicest people I knew.

After a hot, lazy shower, I took a long, deep nap, secure in the conclusion that at least Teresa and I had Lolly's Taco Shack, and that would have to be enough.

Life apparently cannot go on without access to a telephone line: restaurant reservations, baseball tickets, pickup orders of groceries and booze. My second wife had to have a phone nearby; it was essential for her well-being, her sanity. It was so bad that if I wanted to whisper sweet nothings in her ear, I had to call. Except for the occasional need for a client to call me, I doubt I would have a phone at the house. I resent having to wake up to the jarring ringing of a call that sounds urgent but turns out to be another sales pitch for siding, or the latest poll on abortion. I resent talking to people simply because they decided to interrupt me at my home. I lay on my bed, my hand shielding my eyes from the late-afternoon glare, and debated with myself about what to do with the call. Before I could shake my head clear, the answering machine took over and I heard myself monotonously ask the caller to leave a message—I would respond as soon as I could.

"Louie. This is Orlando. I need to talk to you, soon, about that old business, again. Call me at the center, or later tonight at my place. Call me, bro. Don't space me out."

That old business. I didn't want to talk to Orlie Martinez about anything, but I knew I would have to sooner or later. I drifted back to sleep, not sure whether I had dreamed Orlie's voice, not sure whether I was having another nightmare about the old business.

Saturday found me at my office diligently plowing through the work I had neglected the day before. A few divorce pleadings, a letter to a social worker requesting a custody evaluation for the Jimenez kids, a final read-through of the Toltec Records, Inc., bankruptcy papers.

Old Gregorio Leyba landed on his feet no matter what he stumbled into. He was sure the financial collapse of his record store was only a minor obstacle in the way of his slow but steady climb to financial independence. "Bankruptcy is merely another business expense," he told me as he wrote out a check for my two-thousand-dollar retainer and agreed to pay one hundred dollars an hour for anything over twenty hours.

Gregorio had knocked around the Northside for at

least thirty years, from one scam to another. One year he was a bookie in a booth at the back of Romano's Restaurant, the next he had a gig as an antigang "counselor" at a police storefront. Toltec Records was his latest endeavor, and for a time I thought he would pull it off—hawking Mexican and other Latin and Chicano music, as well as tourist curios and gewgaws he imported from Juárez. His customers came from the small but steady stream of workers, refugees, and hustlers from across the border, legal and otherwise.

"Toltec will endure," he assured me. "Give me some time, Montez. Breathing space so I can catch up a bit." The filing of the Chapter 11 provided the time, although it had been a bitch trying to understand his accounts. Leyba did not keep books, paid no taxes, and had no idea of what made up his inventory. He owed me for another ten hours for sifting through his notes, scraps of paper, and telephone messages so I could manufacture a picture of what the hell he had done for the last eighteen months.

The paperwork eventually bored me and I stopped for an early lunch. I usually ate at Mama's Cocina, a hole-in-the-wall around the corner from my office, near the courthouse. I discovered it was closed weekends. I walked to the downtown mall and settled for a tasteless fish sandwich at one of the hamburger chains.

It was my week for blasts from the past. Judge Garcia sat in one of the booths. He smiled when I set my food tray next to his.

"Luis. I was thinking about you. How's business?"

"Business is the pits, Hector. As usual. How's the judge racket?"

Hector was taller than I, more distinguished-looking. His hair had thinned considerably since the days when he wore it down to his shoulders. A patch of sunburned skin lay exposed at the top of his head. Tailored suits and designer shirts had replaced the fringed leather jacket that had been his trademark in college.

"Pues, tu sabes. A racket is a racket, no matter what else it's supposed to be. Look at me. Saturday afternoon. I'm sweating through cases set for Monday morning and I have to finish up what I couldn't get to on Friday. I don't need this, Luis." I nodded. That's what judges are supposed to say. "I heard about Arriega. Too bad. But, I did tell you."

"Yeah, you did. What do I know?" I didn't want to talk about the trial. "I saw Tino the other night. He didn't ask about you."

"That guy! He called me a few weeks ago. He was stopped on Speer doing about eighty-five, wanted me to fix the ticket. Fix the damn ticket! Can you imagine that? What's wrong with him? He never had any sense."

"You took care of him, right?"

The judge looked at his half-eaten sandwich and pushed it away. "I did what I could. I couldn't erase the fucking thing, but I helped him out. You know I would."

Yes. I knew the judge would do what he could for Tino, or me, or any of the brothers from the movement. There was always the movement.

"Orlie called. Any idea what that's about?"

"Could be anything. Who knows with Martinez? On the brink, too many hassles in his job at the center. Gangs and dope and toxic waste from the refinery and all the *mierda* a guy like Orlie can dig up in the barrio. He probably needs legal advice about suing the city because of asbestos in the schools or lead in the water. Sounds like you've been to a reunion. Old names from our flaming youth."

"Don't remind me. With Tino, it wasn't so bad, actually. I met this woman he was with. . . ." Garcia rolled his eyes. "No, no, she was really good-looking. Maybe you know her. She's hooked up with Graves, Snider."

"You don't mean Teresa Fuentes?" The way he said it made me stop for an eye blink. Maybe I didn't mean Teresa Fuentes. "You and women, Luis. You amaze me, hombre." He chuckled like a choking hen. The wheels turned. He flashed on one of the legends from our youth, a story about a wild orgy, a drunken debauchery that had been told and retold so many times over marijuana joints and cheap wine that it now existed only as a steamy mix of fantasy and hallucination.

I yanked him back to the present. "Fuentes, Hector. What about her?"

The smirk stayed on his face. "I gave her a reference, talked to a couple of the partners at Graves, Snider for her. I met her when I taught a summer course at the University of Texas. She was one of my students, man." He laughed, and I couldn't help it—I was jealous. My frown made him laugh that much harder. "Relax, Luis. When I knew her, she was involved with one of her professors, a guy who taught

20

constitutional law. She was the scandal of the school, but the administration loved her. Top grades, excellent writer. Able to argue her way out of the trickiest situation. She aced my class, and that was without any favors."

Hector had taught since he was an undergraduate student. He graduated cum laude, had no trouble in law school. His standards were high and he expected students to sweat out his courses. I had never heard of anyone who had aced one of his classes.

"I've met her only once, and she was with Pacheco. That's all I know about her."

"Tino doesn't seem her type. Oh well. I've seen her only a few times since she showed up here. Surprised the hell out of me when she called for help with the law firm. I'm not exactly the most appropriate person for Graves, Snider. Their lawyers don't appear in my court too often. But I did what I could. She was a remarkable student."

"She seemed bright." Right. As if I gave a damn about her GPA. "We had a few drinks."

"As usual."

"She was a looker. A little young for me, but sweet."

"Sounds like you fell for her. Too young, my ass! You'd jump at the chance." He turned serious and cleared his throat. "I have to tell you, Luis. She was cold-blooded in school. Sharp, articulate, all that. A Chicana who, I have to admit it, I had a few fantasies about. But she did what was necessary for what she wanted. She wasn't very popular with the other students. Too uptight, too *intense* is the word, I guess.

She rubbed people the wrong way. You know the type."

How about anyone who took on any of the causes we embraced with the righteous fervor of kids who thought they could change the world and live forever, too? I let it stay there. I decided I wasn't curious enough for all the dirt about Teresa that Garcia might know. I tossed the rest of my sandwich in the trash bin and promised to call him as soon as I could. I mentioned to him that I was about at the end of my rope, businesswise. He dismissed my remarks as typical sole-practitioner whining.

I worked late that night, rewriting paragraphs of settlement agreements, business leases, and bankruptcy pleadings. I forgot to call Orlie. And every few minutes, Teresa's image floated across my mind and then that of her professor boyfriend and Tino and the judge. What was this? I was a veteran of my own love wars and about ready to throw in the towel for practicing law. Teresa Fuentes was obviously ambitious, an intelligent human being. A Yuppie, if I wanted to be childish about categorizing her. If Garcia was right in his judgment of her, she wouldn't waste any time with a guy like me. We had nothing in common. Well, we were lawyers.

I wrestled with my paperwork, trying to find a sense of purpose, hoping that inspiration would come to me and I would know, *al fin*, what I was supposed to be doing, what I would be when I sat back and said, "Okay, Montez, this is your life and here's what it's about." Behind every word in the contracts, across the figures I penciled in for the latest changes to old man Leyba's bankruptcy papers, and in the corners of my dark office, Teresa Fuentes danced like a ghost. Excuses for calling her popped into my head and, by the time I called it a night, I was scripting scenarios for a meeting with the dark-eyed, black-haired uptown lawyer.

3

I visited the old man on Sunday. Jesús Genaro Montez, migrant worker, coal miner, construction laborer, father of four sons and three daughters, admired and respected by his friends and neighbors, feared by his children. He outlived my mother and I knew he would stand laughing over my coffin when I cashed in.

Scratchy Mexican songs blared from his beat-up phonograph in the tidy, small house on the Westside. I had to turn it down a notch or two merely to talk to him. He shook his head and muttered a few cuss words in Spanish.

He stared at me from his threadbare rocker.

I tried to sound like a concerned son. "You been eating? You want some lunch? We can eat if you want."

He waved his wrinkled, grayed-haired wrist at me in a gesture of disgust at my vile suggestion. "*¿Comida? Todavía, hambre, hambre.* Why don't you eat before you go out, Louie? I can't go gallivanting all around town with you to your taco and burrito joints. I have enough gas as it is." I knew he would fart to demonstrate his point.

"Come on, Dad. Be cool, man. It was a suggestion. I'm not hungry."

"And tell your clients to quit bothering me here at my house. I ain't your secretary."

"What's that about? Who called? When?"

"I don't know when. God, I barely know what today is, much less when some drug dealer or wife beater called to talk to you. Rude, too. *Manito baboso*. They're all alike."

"Dad, Dad. Who called? I don't tell any of my clients to call here for me. And try to remember when."

He tossed a piece of paper at me. It was his note of the telephone message. I couldn't read his scrawl except for a few numbers.

"You know I can't understand your writing. What is this?"

He grabbed the paper and stuck it under his left eye. "Orlie Martinez wants you to call him. Plain as day. Damn."

Orlie really did have to talk to me if he was leaving messages with my father.

"I'm sorry he called here. I didn't give him your number."

"Another lawyer. Why can't he call you at your office like all the others?"

"He's not a lawyer, Dad. A guy I know from college. Did he say what he wanted?"

"Hell. I don't know. Something about an old deal or old work or old *caca*."

"The old business?"

"Yeah. That was it. That's why I thought he was a client or a lawyer. If he wanted to talk about old business, it must be your law stuff. No?"

"No, Dad. This is very old business, something that should have finished long ago. I guess I better go see him."

I promised my father that I would check on him later in the week. He didn't seem to care.

It was a beautiful Sunday. The Zephyrs were playing their last home game of the season and what I needed was to spend the afternoon at the stadium, sweating along the third-base line and pouring beer down my throat for a long nine innings.

It took me fifteen minutes to drive to Five Points, the area traditionally thought of as the black neighborhood. But for years, a unique strain of Chicanos had lived and worked there, with their own style and traditions.

Orlie had chosen the neighborhood for his base of operations because he liked the mix. He ran the Zachary Thompson Community Center with hard work and guts. He carried on antigang, antidrug, and literacy projects in the scruffy building, and coached one of the best basketball teams in the annual city tournament. The center had his total commitment. It was his life. As I drove up to the building, it looked like it might mean his death.

Three guys dressed in baseball caps and neon tank tops, and T-shirts with sports logos had their arms wrapped around Orlie. Another guy, wearing a yellow shirt and pants, slapped him around. Orlie's face was bleeding.

I jerked the car to a stop and jumped out.

"Let him go! Let him go!"

I didn't know what I was going to do, but I had to come up with something. They continued to man-handle Orlie. I took a leap at Yellow Shirt. One of his henchmen grabbed my shoulders and socked me in the face. A dozen punches landed on my body and I fell to my knees. I heard the thuds of the continuing attack on Orlie. I tried to pull myself off the street, when a foot in a hundred-dollar tennis shoe kicked me in the side. I coughed and wheezed, then collapsed to the ground. Orlie fell beside me and we lay there, bleeding, groveling in the dirt. The men ran through the parking lot.

As he climbed into his car, the leader shouted, "One more week, Martinez! One more week!"

I worked hard at breathing. People ran out of the building. A woman who worked in the center brought a towel and tried to clean us up. A couple of boys helped us to our feet. They carried us inside, where they dumped us in the closet Orlie used for an office. He insisted that no cops be called. We received a little first aid and finally we were alone.

Orlie didn't want to complain to the police. I wasn't sure what I should do. I didn't want the thugs to walk away with their gangster tactics. On the other hand, I had to respect Orlie's position. His work in the community might be hurt if he snitched. He had to take care of the problem himself.

He brushed his hair straight back from his high forehead. He wore jeans and a flannel shirt and the penny loafers he latched on to in college and never could forsake, not even at the height of his revolutionary mania. He looked as if he had lost weight.

27

"What the hell does Hummy Gonzales want with you?"

"He's a punk. A dealer. You name it. He doesn't like what we do here in the center, so he wants us to stop. He threatens us all the time. I'm not worried about him."

"Is that why you've been calling me? Humberto Gonzales is muscling you?"

"No, Louie. It's more than that. It's Rocky. I've had phone calls, threats. . . ."

"Damn you, Orlie. It's been twenty years, and you won't let it go. Give it a rest."

He paced around the cubicle, smoking a cigarette, a habit I thought he had given up years before.

"This is different, Louie. This guy says I'm next, that it's not finished. That there are more of us who have to pay."

"It's a crank, Orlie. It could be anybody who knows about that, to scare you into something. It could be Hummy, for all you know."

"This weirdo said things. Things that only those who were there that night could know. He talked about the guys in the white hoods, the creek by the road where Rocky was shot. He knows that Tino and Hector were there. He said we were all going to end up the same way as Rocky. I don't think it's a crank call."

Orlie had always been tough. He was short and skinny, but he had heart when it counted. Simply sticking it out at the center took more strength than I had mustered in several years. But now he was scared. He smoked one cigarette after another. His eyes jumped around the room and his eyelids twitched every few seconds. I had seen him like this one other time—the night Rocky Ruiz was shotgunned to death by masked and hooded men on a dark country road, twenty years before.

It wasn't an accident that Rocky, Orlie, and I had teamed up. The number of black and brown students at the university could be counted on two hands. We three survived by leaning on one another after we shook off the trauma of finding ourselves surrounded and outflanked by Anglo professors and students. From final exams to self-defense in cowboy bars, we counted on our combined strength for support and protection. We moved on from the immature pranks of our freshman year to the heady business of Chicano liberation by the time we were ready to graduate—marches, demonstrations, building take-overs, conferences. Arm in arm, we rode the wave of Chicano pride and enthusiasm that swept the Southwest for a few short years.

We joined the United Mexican American Students. We made demands for ethnic studies and minority-student recruitment. But there was more going on in the revolution. Rocky, Hector, Orlie, Tino, and a few others created a secret group they called Los Guerilleros, although Rocky preferred to call himself one of the Gorillas. They adopted an identity created by the red berets they wore at movement functions.

They molded a world where they were the protectors of the people, the vanguard of the revolution. They practiced karate, studied the lives of Che Guevara and the Flores-Magón brothers, and wore military-style clothing. They acted as security at demonstrations and meetings and, once or twice, they helped keep things cool and under control when cops or rednecks baited the crowd. I sat in on some of their meetings, but I never wore the beret. I never passed the test, whatever it was, and they and I accepted the fact that because I was on the outside of what they were doing, I could serve as an anchor, a sounding wall to help keep them somewhere near reality.

They were my best friends, but they lived part of their lives locked away from me, haranguing one another about the direction of the movement, the mistakes of the leaders, the truth about Vietnam or the Black Panthers. I was too much of a loner and a cynic and I let them know I thought some of what they did was childish. They indulged me. We had been friends too long, been through too many close calls to let a little thing like a revolution splinter us.

"Take it easy, Orlie. Why would anyone care about you and Rocky and the others now? Twenty years is a long time to wait to finish something like that. It doesn't make sense."

He tossed his cigarette on the floor and stamped it out with his boot. "Fuck you, Louie. I don't care if it sounds crazy. All I know is that a phone kook told me the job wasn't finished. We have to find out who it is, and stop him."

I guess I knew I had a part in this. Orlie's directive didn't surprise me. Orlie had duly impressed me in college. He had me figured out early on. He was the leader, the driving force behind much of what we did as students. He talked to us about incidents from around the country, showed us magazines and pamphlets from groups in Los Angeles and San Francisco, made sure we were aware of the latest confrontations. He was a step ahead of the rest of us, a hard-liner, with little patience for people who failed to see the correctness of his line as soon as he presented it.

"I saw Hector yesterday. He didn't say anything about this. Why just you? Why no calls to the other guys? Someone's rattling your cage, trying to spook you. Make you do something crazy, Orlie. Get a grip, man."

"Yeah, well, I'm spooked. The motherfucker got to me. I saw Rocky blown away that night, Louie. I heard the killers laughing while Rocky lay bleeding to death in the dirt. I heard them talking about who was next. I'll do whatever's necessary to stop them. I'll need your help. It ain't finished yet."

I had tried to tell myself over the years that it *was* over, that it had been finished that night. But the drops of sweat rolling down Orlie's face brought it all back, with all the pain and tears, the grief and sadness I had locked away with my youth.

We had helped organize a conference of student groups from around the state. The event was marred with factional fighting, turf disputes, and maneuvering for leadership of a movement that had lost its direction. The last night of the conference was a disaster. Some of the groups stormed out of the meetings. There were shouts of "sellouts, *¡vendidos!*" Arguments erupted over whether to vote for Chicano candidates in local elections if they ran as Democrats. Women angrily demanded time to polemicize about the problem with machismo. A haggard quartet of intellectuals talked about the need to work toward the creation of a new Communist party that would take care of the needs of "national minorities." They were booed off the podium.

We had met at Orlie's apartment late that night. A depressed, worn-out mood covered us. I drank a few beers and made a clumsy exit. Orlie and Rocky were in the middle of an argument over Chicano capitalism versus Third World unity, and I couldn't take it anymore.

They drove into the scrub country in the eastern part of the county, drinking beer and smoking marijuana. The excuse for the drive was to watch the sun rise, one of Orlie's methods for uniting people. Hector told me later that no one except Orlie really was up for the long wait until morning. They were too burned out, too drunk and tired. As usual, they gave in to Orlie's spiel that they needed to stride forward when it looked like the situation was hopeless. If Los Guerilleros couldn't maintain, how could the people endure, how could they expect the masses to join in the struggle?

The hooded men showed up in pickups. They had no trouble subduing the wasted band of revolutionaries. They taunted the Chicanos with racial slurs, beat Rocky with the butt of a rifle. They wanted to teach the wetbacks a lesson. Rocky freaked out, couldn't handle it. He ran. They shot him in the back with a shotgun. It wasn't clear what happened after that. Either the killers panicked and drove away or Orlie, Hector, and Tino managed to escape in the darkness during the horror of Rocky's dying.

Rocky's death ended the movement for most of us.

A grand-jury investigation made plenty of headlines, dragged on for months. No one was indicted. There were stories about the Ku Klux Klan and the Posse Comitatus and whispered rumors about a hit by a rival Chicano group. Some said the police had removed the ablest young Chicano, and others said he died because he was high on drugs and alcohol.

On the day after his death, I searched the place where Rocky Ruiz died, dried tears on my face, fear taking root deep in my heart. I found only bits of clothing, bloodstains on the rocks, and dozens of policemen warily watching my every step.

I tried to reassure Margarita, Rocky's wife, and Victoria, their daughter, too young to understand yet terrified by her mother's grief. Margarita had avoided Rocky's politics and his death severed whatever tenuous ties she had with the movement. She took his body to Texas and buried him next to his mother. She didn't stay for the memorial march held in his honor two days after his killing.

Orlie disappeared. I heard he was in Los Angeles, trying to politicize factory workers. He showed up in Denver after a few years—earnest, continuing the good fight, struggling for the rights of the oppressed. He worked his way up to running the community center. He served on a half a dozen task forces and community groups, his fingers in every progressive pie. Powerful people called on him for his views, yet he lived on the lip of poverty, inundated by whatever was his latest project and the dozens of headaches the center gave him each day. I respected the man, but I couldn't shake the feeling that he was a drag to be around. Too many schemes that didn't work, too much rhetoric, and not enough time to sit back and check things out. He made me feel guilty. Our relationship had been reduced to an occasional phone call or office visit when he needed quick legal advice about one of his causes.

As I drove away from the center, I remembered the excitement, the frenzy that he brought to any project. He quickly assumed the role of the group's core. He had had his time in the spotlight, and then some. I couldn't help but wonder whether Orlie didn't welcome the latest threats, whether he didn't see them as vindication of his fights—the movement—his entire life. Once more, he had purpose, pressure, and a life-and-death situation on his hands, exactly like the old days.

4

I made it into the clinic by seven the next morning. Bruised ribs and torn cartilage. The pretty physician's assistant did not take long to attend to my wounds. She wrapped my rib cage, pushed and poked various body parts, and generally made me squirm on the examination room's paper-covered bed. She also managed to ask about my age, weight, and exercise and drinking habits—topics I'm not fond of talking about in public. She said I had to take it easy for at least ten days. Right. I was buried with the work I avoided during Arriega's trial; Orlie wanted me to help figure out what was going on with the psycho phone calls; it was Monday morning and I had to hustle new business for the rest of the week if I hoped to stay even with my creditors. And I was supposed to lounge around for a week and a half.

I popped a couple of painkillers at the office. The assistant had balked at first, but my whining won her over and eventually she wrote out a prescription for oxycodone something or other. It wasn't as if I was a druggie mooching handouts for my habit. As she handed me the prescription, she cooed in her best professional manner. "Take it easy with these. Follow the directions on the bottle. No alcohol. One tablet every six hours, not on an empty stomach, but don't eat too much. They might cause nausea." Filling the prescription was the only bit of advice I remembered.

The trial hung on me like a suit of chain mail. I had devoted Saturday to trying to catch up. The light workout at the center with Hummy Gonzales and his aerobics boys hadn't refreshed me. Breathing was pain.

But there was nowhere else for me that morning. If I didn't go into work, I would have to take care of the dozens of odd jobs I had neglected around the house, like the toilet that wouldn't quit flushing. Or arrange a visit with the boys, and I was sure they and their mother hadn't noticed that I hadn't been by in a few weeks. The office seemed to be the lesser of a couple of evils.

I told Evangelina to hold my calls while I prepared for the Armstrong hearing. Donna Armstrong was an old client of mine. The first time I represented her, I was a legal-aid lawyer. Somehow, I had been her attorney ever since. She was a black woman with eight or nine kids, two or three ex-husbands, and more problems than any other person I knew. I helped her with divorces, child support, cleaning up the details left by a husband who kicked over while driving a cab, and a half a dozen minor criminal cases filed against two of her sons. The latest hassle was an eviction. She had been served with a demand to vacate the house she had lived in for years. She didn't understand it and insisted I help her. I tried to refer the case to legal aid, but Evangelina found Mrs. Armstrong curled up on the building's steps when she unlocked the office. She had a court appearance that morning. I wasn't prepared and I didn't feel as if I could do anything for her. Naturally, at 9:30 I found myself staring into the red and bulging face of the Honorable Martin Grant while he gave Mrs. Armstrong justice.

"Order! There will be order in this court!" The judge's dry throat constricted around his words. His pink hands, clutching a shiny new gavel, were flushed and hot. He pounded the gavel on the top of his dark, deeply grained judicial bench to emphasize his frustration with the proceedings. "If you can't control your client, Mr. Montez, I'll have the both of you taken from the courtroom by my bailiff! Do you understand, Mr. Montez?"

I mumbled under my breath. "Hell, yes, I understand!" I had my arms wrapped around Mrs. Armstrong, no easy task considering that she weighed almost three hundred pounds and her forearms were as big as my neck. "I'm trying, Your Honor! Maybe your bailiff can give me a hand?" Mrs. Armstrong twisted and turned like a wounded bull, doing all she could to throw me off her back. She heaved and screamed, shaking her fist at the judge, the plaintiff, and the plaintiff's attorney.

"You ain't throwin' me outta my home, no fuckin' way. I got my rights!" She jerked free and swung her meaty right fist at me. She caught me on the chin and knocked me back into the bailiff, who had fi-

37

nally decided to help. We tripped each other and fell onto the courtroom floor.

Harold Hoskins was scared. The landlord, real estate investor, and upright member of a dozen different boards of directors of prestigious and philanthropic organizations wanted Mrs. Armstrong and her kids out and gone. He had plans for the block where her ramshackle three-bedroom house sat among parking lots and deserted buildings. Hoskins had given her thirty days, more than his attorney, Gaston Peters, told him he had to, and then she went and asked for her day in court and he was forced to waste practically an entire morning.

Judge Grant understood the economics of development. He knew that the big picture meant she had to disappear. It didn't matter how long she had lived there. It didn't matter how many kids she had or how difficult it was for her to find another place with cheap rent and close access to the bus routes. All that really mattered, according to the judge, was that she didn't have a lease and so she had to leave when the landlord said she had to.

"Lease! Are you fuckin' crazy! I been there for ten years, with about fifty different landlords. I don't even know who this little shriveled-up cracker is!" She shook a beefy hand in the direction of Hoskins. "I ain't never talked to him before! I been lucky to see receipts for my rent, much less no fuckin' lease."

The judge shouted at her to sit down and shut up. She responded by moving toward the judge's bench, and that was when I grabbed her and held on for my life until she punched her way free.

She bounced across the floor to the plaintiff's

table, where Hoskins and Peters watched her approach, like ants before a tank. My sore ribs kept me on the courtroom floor, cringing in pain. I saw her gigantic back advancing on the two men.

"Mothafuckas! Mothafuckas!" She smashed her fists into their faces and they went sprawling back into the knee-high railing that separated the attorneys and judge from the rabble in the courtroom pews.

Grant jerked to his feet, hammering his gavel, screaming at the top of his lungs. "Order! Order! Order!" His voice cracked as he squeaked out one more "Order!" The gavel broke in his hands. His face drooped and he sat down.

The bailiff charged after Mrs. Armstrong. She stood ready for him. He attacked, but she fended him off with quick, deadly jabs. A trio of deputy sheriffs ran into the courtroom, their clubs drawn. They stared for an instant, not believing what they saw, and, I couldn't help it, I thought of the Three Stooges. They jumped into the free-for-all and the entire group—a swirling, gyrating ball of cussing, screaming humanity—rolled out the courtroom. They broke the thick green glass in the door, activating the alarm. A high-pitched ringing echoed through the courthouse, down the dark and tunnel-like hallways, and clerks, attorneys, defendants and plaintiffs, judges and cops thought a fire had finally started in the battered old building. People poured from the courthouse.

I grunted and picked myself off the floor. I hunted down Mrs. Armstrong's file folder. Hoskins lay unconscious on the floor. His attorney was on one knee, rubbing his bruised jaw. I stuffed the file in my briefcase. "Look, Peters, if you want to work something out, we can talk. Give me a call. The ten o'clock news would love to hear about how you and your client are throwing out the old widow lady and her batch of kids. Maybe you have another place for her, eh?" I tried to sound serious, but he was a silly-looking creep. I laughed as I talked.

Peters's face darkened to a deep plum red hue. "You son of a bitch. I'm gonna sue you and your client for everything I can dig out of you. You're gonna hear from *my* lawyer, Montez. You'll regret the day you decided to represent that animal. You'll pay for this, Montez, you'll pay!"

I looked back at the judge. Grant held his face in his hands as he bent over the remains of his gavel. I thought I saw tears on the judge's cheeks.

I marched out of the courthouse with the rest of the refugees. The Armstrong eviction was the best time I'd had on a case in a long time. I rubbed the ball of my thumb across my eyes to dry my own tears. It really had been a good case.

The crowd on the courthouse lawn was not sure what to do with itself. Talkative groups of clerks and bailiffs laughed uneasily, like kids playing hooky. I acknowledged the court staff and attorneys I recognized. I soaked up the crowd's excitement, the rush created when something totally unexpected disrupts the day's routine and there isn't anything you can do about it.

Off by himself was Judge Garcia, amused by the scene at the courthouse, his arms folded across his chest. His impressive stature looked out of place in the middle of the chaos.

He waved for me to join him. "I heard this was the work of one of your clients. *¡Mano!* Your client attacked Grant, or something like that? Your reputation is shot around here." As an afterthought, he added, "You sick? You look kind of pale."

I could feel the truth in his words. His sarcasm was meant to be light, but it was clear to me that my career wasn't panning out. In less than a week, I had lost two cases. Hell, in less than twenty-four hours I had been knocked around and laid out flat on my butt by two different people. It wasn't Monday noon yet.

"You're only as good as your last case, Hector. You know that. Unfortunately, my last case cleared out the courthouse." Sirens interrupted us as fire trucks screamed around the corner. Policemen rerouted traffic. A couple of intersections jammed. The chief clerk tried to explain to one of the firemen that it was only a broken door. It did no good. A crew of firemen ran up the steps, dragging hoses and carrying axes. They had to assure themselves that the public was safe. Mrs. Armstrong's struggle for justice had seriously delayed, if not completely halted, the justice system.

"Hector, I need to talk to you."

"Yeah. Nothing's happening here, at least for a while."

We ran across the street, dodging the fire trucks, police cars, and winding hoses, and sat down on one of the park benches usually occupied by a sleeping

41

transient but currently empty because of the up-roar.

"Has Orlie called you?"

"I haven't talked with him in months. You said he had been trying to reach you. I guess he did."

"He reached me. And you know what it's about."

He nodded. "Rocky. What else?"

I told Hector Garcia about the telephone threats, the fight with Hummy Gonzales, my sore ribs, and Orlie's whacked-out state of mind. I asked whether Hector had heard anything.

"No, Louie. The only time Rocky's name comes up is when I see you or Orlie or Tino. Nobody's called me. Nobody's threatened me. I haven't heard about any white hoods or finishing the job or anything like that. It's only someone trying to scare Orlie." He spat out the words as if they were pieces of rotten meat. He resented the idea that the death of Rocky Ruiz could once again be part of his life.

"Orlie is taking this thing seriously, Hector. He really thinks that—"

The judge stood, stopping me in midsentence. "That's crazy! He can't, he knows . . . Fuck! It's a prank, Louie. Leave it at that. Don't drag up old ghosts. None of us really wants that." I thought he would say more, but he glanced at his watch and changed his tone. "I have to go. Need to figure out what happens with today's docket. I'll call." He ran off and disappeared in the crowd.

I sat on the bench, the late-summer sun heating up my suit, sweat clinging to the edge of my collar. I refrained from scratching at the tape around my torso. There was another itch threatening my comfort level, a torment in my skull that I could reach only if I called on strength I seemed to remember from days when risks and gambles were accepted parts of life and life would last forever. That memory faded, however, and eventually, when I tired of watching the confusion across the street, I walked back to my office, carrying a weight I did not understand. My brain would not accept the images thrust on it by my old friends.

I had a hard time picturing the killing from twenty years ago in the same set with men such as Judge Garcia and Orlie Martinez. It was too long ago, back when we were different people, when the world was lost in confusion and hatred, when the nightmares were only bad drug trips and a *carnal* could talk you down almost any night.

Evangelina stopped me as soon as I walked in the reception area. "Louie, you look terrible. What happened?"

"Funny how people keep telling me how bad I look. I think Mrs. Armstrong finally fired me. She lost it in the courtroom. They dragged her away. I guess we should check on her, make sure she's going to be okay. All those kids."

"I'll call the sheriff, see where they ended up taking her. But what's wrong with you? Are you all right?"

"About usual." The office closed in around me and I knew I was lying. I had to leave. "I hate to do this to you, Evie. I'll try to make it back after lunch." I threw a few files and legal pads in my briefcase. I handed the Armstrong file to Evangelina and asked her to cancel my appointments. She stared after me as I rushed away, not bothering to ask any questions.

I drove in the general direction of my house, not sure what the plan was for dealing with my general burnout. I almost convinced myself that I should give Teresa a call. Maybe some time with her would lift me out of whatever I had sunk into. I flipped on the car radio with the hope that the right kind of music would help. The courthouse evacuation had made the noon news. And so had the discovery of Tino Pacheco's body under a viaduct near the Platte River. Or, rather, the discovery of what was left of Tino after the shotgun finished its work.

5

Teresa's black dress emphasized her dark skin. Her hair stretched back in a tight bun. She stood near the open grave, her slender body outlined in gold by the sun. Quiet, calm, always in control. She looked better than I remembered. As I prayed for Tino's forgiveness for all the cheap shots I'd taken at him, I managed to throw in a bit of thanks for the last introduction he made for me.

The violence of men can turn the basic fact of death complicated. It should have been a simple affair—Tino died, his friends and enemies grieved, and he was buried and laid to rest. Yet almost a week had passed since Tino's killing and his coffin remained in the sunlight, not covered by damp earth and solemn prayers. The autopsy and police investigation delayed everything, including the public mourning.

A short article appeared in the newspapers, without any mention of a possible connection between Tino's and Rocky's deaths. Hector's phone calls were frantic, but I couldn't pull it together to see him. I told myself I needed time to sort out the situation, to stand back and piece together an explanation that would not answer all the questions but at least might make me feel better about burying Tino. If only I had the time. I was dragged into the rush of events and I never did feel better about Tino's funeral.

I had convinced Orlie to talk to the police about the threats. He insisted I go with him. We retold the story of Rocky Ruiz. A couple of the cops remembered Rocky's murder, but they doubted that the two killings had anything to do with each other. It was too logical for the detectives and they wanted to check out Hummy Gonzales—they loved to check out Hummy Gonzales, although Orlie hadn't given any details about his problems with the dealer and all-around bad actor. The telephone threats were "part of the file" and there was no official theory yet on why Tino had been killed. My impression was that the police were willing to let it go as merely another rumble between Chicanos. Tino's penchant for arguments and fights was mentioned a few times at the police station.

The crowd of mourners was a strange mix. Hector and Orlie and a few other Chicanos who had known Tino for years shuffled nervously in the shade of a tree. A group of his tenants, young women, huddled in a knot away from the rest of us, whispering and crying. I concluded they were Tino's favorites in the apartment building. Two men, one black, one white, with sport coats, open collars, and fancy shoes, hovered in the background. They arrived late and left early.

A few cops tried to look inconspicuous. It was obvious to all of us when one of them followed the well-dressed salt-and-pepper set.

The priest's mumbo jumbo ended and they lowered the casket into the earth. Orlie jumped when the pulleys and ropes ground out their sad duty. I put my arm around his shoulders, more to steady him than anything else. Through it all, he was a mess. Uptight, scared, a freak-out waiting to happen.

Judge Garcia, on the other hand, had come apart. I had doubted that he would attend the funeral, but he surprised me. His neat, expensive dark suit contrasted sharply with the edgy condition of his eyes. He cornered me at the church when we lined up to serve as pallbearers.

"I need to talk to Orlie. Maybe the three of us should get together, try to think this through." I promised him we would, but no time was set for the meeting.

Tino's only relative was a sister who lived in the southern part of the state. She asked me to say a few words about Tino because she thought we were good friends. She had bailed us out of jail once. That said something about our relationship.

I waited until the priest packed away his gear. Without an introduction, I said my good-bye to Tino Pacheco.

"The last time I saw Tino was at the end of a wild night, and that's the way I will remember him. Some of us here knew him when we were kids. We grew up with one another, in a time when ideas and ideals were tossed around like we would never run out of them, and sometimes we got carried away with emotion and recklessness. But it was from the heart, whether we wanted justice or peace or love or a party. Tino was always in the middle of it. He would never shy away from a fight, and we depended on him when we needed strength. I don't know why Tino died. How can anyone make sense out of such an insane thing? Whatever the reason, Tino must have died like a man, and only a coward could have done this."

I started to mishandle the words as memories of Tino flooded over me. I remembered the young tough guy, swaggering around campus, forcing other Chicanos, by his example, to strut their stuff, intimidating those who had nothing to do with the movement, and ultimately challenging himself to reach heights of pride the rest of us could only imagine. I saw him marching with illiterate farm workers, carrying their kids on his shoulders through hot and dusty fields when the college students demonstrated support for the migrants' union-organizing efforts. He wore a bright red bandanna wrapped around his head, the black eagle of the farm workers painted on his T-shirt. And I saw him laughing, slapping one of us on the back, telling us, "Relax, *ese*, it ain't no big thing." My speech drifted apart and I stopped.

Teresa grabbed my upper arm and squeezed. She whispered in my ear. "Tino would have liked that. We can go now."

We made our way back to where the cars were parked.

"There was a time when that guy was as close to me as anybody has ever been. Yet the last several years, I had nothing to do with him. Unless he called me. Then we went out, drank, same old thing. Now I'm the only guy who says anything about him at his funeral."

"He respected you, Luis. He thought you were always straight with him. Honest. That's the word he used. He didn't say that about any of the others."

Judge Garcia and Orlie Martinez climbed into the judge's metallic gray sports car. They were in too much of a hurry. The judge's tires squealed on the asphalt drive out of the cemetery. I expected they would try to call me to set up the meeting that Hector had determined was critical.

Teresa surprised me then. She turned and hugged me. I thought it had something to do with Tino's death, maybe a spontaneous exhibition of sorrow or pain. She had gone out with the guy, after all. He was the first person she had established any kind of relationship with after she relocated to Denver. I hugged back. She ended it quickly and gently pushed me away. Those eyes. The heat, the pain in my ribs, the chaos that surrounded me the last few days, all jammed up in my head and I felt dizzy staring into Teresa's beautiful face. Except for yellow tablets of pain drugs, I hadn't eaten anything decent in days.

"Things catch up to people, Luis. Some faster than others. Maybe Tino was overdue. It all evens out, in the end." She headed for her car.

"Teresa, wait. I need to talk. Think out loud. What if I come over? I don't know what else to do."

She opened her car door, hung a pair of sunglasses across her eyes, and searched for her keys in her purse. I stood on somebody's grave, aware that I looked like I was begging for an answer.

"Follow me, Luis."

I was so wound up, I could hardly talk. She fixed drinks and flipped on a compact disc of Stan Getz. I was surprised. I guess I thought she was too young to be into jazz.

She asked about my practice and I moaned and groaned for a few minutes until I bored myself. Finally, I told her the story about Los Guerilleros and the death of Rocky Ruiz and the telephone calls threatening the life of Orlie Martinez.

"Rocky was the friend you told me about, the guy from Texas? You didn't mention that he was murdered, Luis. Why?"

"I remember Rocky in a different way. It's like his death never really happened. I wasn't there the night they shot him. I guess I never dealt with it. That was the worst time for me. There was this big movement commemoration march. People from all over the state were there, all kinds of activists— Anglos, blacks, Chicanos. We marched through the campus and over to the police station. Everybody gave a speech. Hours of rhetoric. Political babble I didn't care about anymore."

The music ended and Teresa turned off the machine. She added wine to her glass. "What was so special about Ruiz?"

I wanted to come up with a great answer. I wanted to let her know that there once was a person in the world who lived a unique life, who had an effect on the lives of so many others. It wasn't my week to come up with the great speech of my life.

"He was a martyr, a hero. Klansmen or Birchers or cops or provocateurs or the FBI killed him—there were a hundred different theories. And what was strange, ironic, was that a lot of the people making speeches didn't like Rocky, or any of the Berets. There was all this factionalism, a lot of egos in the movement. But I guess we overcame that when he was killed."

"A high price to pay for unity."

"You'll never know, Teresa. This may be rhetoric, but Rocky Ruiz was one of a kind. He had, hell, I don't know, he had a way of understanding, of picking out what was important. He could see things clearly. That's what I remember about Rocky. He could see."

Details I had thought were long forgotten came back to me.

"He talked about building a new culture, not only for Chicanos but for everyone, a new way, he called it. It sounds silly now, but back then we were all thinking about change, about remaking society, and Rocky took it very seriously. And he was a poet. He wrote about the people, *la raza*, sacrifice, and love. He taught himself how to play the guitar. Learned a bunch of Mexican *corridos*, and at parties, sooner or later, he would drag out his instrument and soon we'd be singing away, hollering and dancing. Rocky could do that." Twenty years gone and I mourned for my brother.

"Give me that before you drop it." She took the empty glass I had been waving in the air.

I reached for her. It seemed like the only thing to do right then. I kissed her lips as softly as I could manage. I gathered her into my arms. She rested her head against my shoulder.

The weight I had carried for days loosened its grip. The smoothness of her cheeks rubbed against my lips and I could smell her perfume and the heat of the cemetery trapped in her hair. I rubbed the skin on her neck and arms.

She pulled away. "I, I can't, Luis. Let's not do this. I'm sorry. I shouldn't have kissed you." She turned away. I had been turned down before and I thought I could deal with it. Everyone has the right to say no. This one hurt. I felt old, used up. Who the hell did I think I was?

"I guess I better go. I don't want to give you any problems. I don't know what to say."

Her hand held my chin. She kissed my cheek. "We don't need to say anything. Maybe we can talk another night."

The drive home was uneventful. I carried the feel of her lips on my face, the sensitive touch of her hand on mine. I thought out scenarios of lovemaking that might have been. I imagined dialogue between us, set the stage for an affair that would light up the night with its fire. As I parked the car, I realized the radio was too loud, the brakes were loose and noisy, and I was alone with my dreams and visions and a numb exhaustion that mere sleep would not end.

6

---

*B*efore I could face the pile of deadlines stacked on my desk, I convinced myself I had to have a breakfast burrito and real coffee. Mama's Cocina offered what I needed. I dropped grease and chile on the morning newspaper as I sat in one of the tiny booths along the wall.

The big news item was the baseball election. The citizens had to vote on whether they wanted to foot the bill for a new stadium if the major leagues decided to give Denver a team. For me there was no debate. I already had money saved for season tickets. Baseball offered one of the few opportunities for my sons and I to do something we all enjoyed. Watching the stars of the National League might be a real boost for whatever relationship I maintained with the kids. I couldn't understand the reluctance of some of the people to add to their tax bill. But then, I was willing to pay for baseball. I would have paid whatever the baseball gods asked.

The vote wasn't the only hang-up. There were

plenty of unanswered questions, such as who the owners were going to be, where the stadium would be built, and exactly how much the final bill would be once all the details were added in. I didn't care, but, according to the news story, movers and shakers in the financial community were giving these issues plenty of thought. Heavy pushing and shoving had to be going on behind the scenes.

The story mentioned a small group of investors lobbying for a stadium site in the middle of the Westside barrio. Economic development for the Westside was the rallying cry. It would wipe out the community, of course, but that was nothing new. The entire neighborhood of Auraria, also on the Westside, had been sacrificed for the ugly buildings and parking lots that made up the Auraria Higher Education Complex. Three community colleges on the border of downtown that ostensibly served urban students had at one time seemed like a good return for a handful of old homes and memories owned by people who had lived in the area for generations. If it worked before, it could work again. That was the hit I pulled from the story.

The investors group had generated support because there were a few minorities involved—a couple of Hispanic businessmen, a black politician, and a few others who must have had a trace of Native American blood somewhere along the line. The real money was white, naturally. The up-front guys, the ones smiling all over the first page, had color and unusual names.

The acrid taste of greed mixed in with the eggs, potatoes, and chorizo of my burrito. Baseball was such a simple game and it was becoming as trashy as the rest of the country because there was too damn much money to be made. I left the paper and my used-up napkins and finally went to work.

Evangelina met me at the door.

"You have about a dozen messages from Judge Garcia and Orlie Martinez. Gregorio Leyba needs to see you today. A lawyer named Abrams wants to talk to you about the disruption your client caused in Judge Grant's courtroom. Said he was with the Supreme Court Disciplinary Committee, or something like that. And your father. He called first thing this morning."

I took the pink message slips from her and leafed through them until I came across the note from Dad. It said only to call. Now what?

"Call Leyba for me. Tell him to come in tomorrow morning to sign some papers. About ten. I'll do something with the rest of these."

I said it too quickly, with too much authority, as if I doubted that she knew what I was talking about. I didn't have the concentration to respect the amenities she required. She gave me a look that said, You know what you can do with your damn messages, but she was too hip to actually verbalize her distaste. She had me figured out years before and it was too late for her to try to train me. Hell, it was my practice, my career. I was only a paycheck. There were plenty of lawyers in town who would jump at the chance to have her establish order in their offices.

I dialed my father's number, but there was no answer, and that made me worry. He didn't go out much. Once in a while, he visited old buddies at one of the apartments set up for the elderly, or he had lunch at a seniors center. But those were rare. It seemed to me that the more he aged, the more entrenched his fears became about the terrible things that brown and black and white kids could do to him. He stayed home, puttering around the yard, watching the tube, or playing his records. His grandchildren showed up on weekends and that kept him busy, and he loved it—although to hear him bitch, you wouldn't know what they meant to him. I decided I had to see what was going on with my father, if anything.

I found Evangelina at her desk. She frowned as I approached.

"I'll be back as soon as I can. I don't know for sure how long this will take." More frowning. I needed to take affirmative action. "I'm a little worried about my father. If he calls, can you tell him to stay put in his house until I show up?" The frown softened with a curl of concern. "I appreciate your help, Evangelina. I need all the help I can scrounge up these days." She didn't exactly light up, but I thought I squeaked through.

"I hope your father's all right. I'll cover for you as much as I can."

"Thanks."

I was leaving when she said, "Get some rest, Luis. You look tired." I smiled at her and shrugged my shoulders as if I was the goofiest guy she had had the bad luck to run into and what did I know about taking it easy. I was a busy son of a gun, on the run, with buddies dying and a father not answering the telephone and the Supreme Court questioning my professional integrity. And, oh yeah, the pain in my ribs reminded me that I wasn't much of a boxer.

Jesús Genaro Montez had been entertained by me for as long as I could remember. He had this smile that irked me, but there was nothing I could do about it. He thought it was particularly funny when I came home from college spouting my movement ideology. *Chicano* was a derogatory word as far as he was concerned. "If you want to be called 'boy Mexican,' that's up to you, boy." What made him really laugh was that most of my comrades in the movement did not speak Spanish. What we knew about our culture, we learned from books, ignoring the lessons people such as my father had tried to teach us for years. "What kind of revolution is this if you kids can't even convince your parents? You're lucky to be in America, where they put up with nonsense like this. In Mexico, you would have been lined up and shot the first time you started spouting off about demands. Look what they did at the Olympics." And yet, when Rocky was killed, he was there for me. He found room for me in his house, left me alone while I tried to work out of the depression. When it was time for me to leave, he said only that I could come back whenever I wanted.

My becoming a lawyer embarrassed him. Lawyers were people to avoid. One spoke to an *abogado* only if one had such big trouble that there was no other way. If you failed, you saw a lawyer. And a lawyer made money off of people's misery. It was that simple. Lawyers didn't advise or counsel. They didn't negotiate or represent. They shuttled people in or out of trouble, if the fee was big enough. A client was a person who had been reduced to having no other choice except to see a lawyer. It was a pitiful, miserable world lawyers lived and worked in and it was too bad his youngest son couldn't manage to do something honorable with his life. A carpenter or farmer, for example.

Summer should have eased up, but the temperature stayed in the nineties. The car seats were hot and sticky. I turned on the air conditioner and tried to listen, over the fan, to the jazz station managed by the busiest woman I had ever met. I knew Flo Hernandez from my university days, when the various chapters of the United Mexican American Students gathered to rant and rave about parity and ethnic studies. She had attended the largest school in the state and her group had had a reputation for arrogance. But she made sure things were done. We never imagined, as we downed shots of tequila and wrote our latest sets of demands, that she would end up as the general manager of a public radio station broadcasting traditional American music like jazz, blues, and that good ol' Afro beat. I rarely saw her anymore. She was much too occupied with fundraising drives and special events promoting the station. And I was involved with the death of an old friend while I tripped over the loose ends of my law practice.

I guess I overreacted to my father's telephone message. Maybe I was looking for any excuse that would keep me away from my work and Martinez and the judge. Jesús wasn't an invalid and he certainly never asked for special treatment. I had about talked myself into turning back to my office when I spotted him walking down the street. I pulled over and honked my horn.

He jumped at the sound. His old fedora rolled off the top of his head. At first, he didn't know who I was. Then, as he realized my identity, I could see the small brushfire in his eyes. He picked up his hat and whacked it against his leg. Years of dust exploded around him.

"What the hell are you doing? *¡Válgame Dios!* Son of a bitch! You almost gave me a heart attack. Don't you know better than to sneak up on an old man and blare your goddamn horn at him? What are you doing out here, anyway?"

"Calm down, or you *will* have a heart attack. You called me. You didn't answer the phone, so I, huh, I . . ."

"You thought I was in trouble or lying in a gutter someplace. Something morbid like that, no? I'm not senile yet, Louie."

He walked around the car and climbed into the front seat. Apparently, I was giving him a ride wherever it was he was going.

"What's up, Dad? What are you doing out here? And why did you call?"

"I need a reason to call my big-shot lawyer son? I can't just want to talk, maybe see how he's doing? *Sin vergüenza!* You should be ashamed."

"Where to?"

"The grocery store, where else? Need some dog food for dinner."

I gave him a disgusted look. "Don't fool around, Dad."

"What do you expect? You act like I'm a *viejito loco*. Like I should be in one of those homes pissing all over myself."

"Okay, Dad. You made your point. I'll take you to the store. Is that why you called?"

"*¿Qué crees?* Of course. I needed a ride." His eyes followed a woman crossing the intersection. "Plus, I heard about that friend of yours, Pacheco. I met him, no? The big guy, real *mal hombre, sí?* I thought maybe you needed some help, with the arrangements or something. *Tu sabes.*"

I smiled at the old man. "Yeah, Dad. I know. Thanks for offering."

I drove him to a glossy chain store and waited in the car while he bought what he thought were essentials. The jazz station took me away with a nice set of music that included Miles Davis, Paquito D'Rivera, and Sweets Edison. Crystal-clear visions of making love with Teresa floated in the car. I was too old for this, I thought, but there I was, daydreaming about lips and smooth shoulder skin, my fingers wrapped in strands of her long hair, words of lust and tenderness whispered in my ear. I worked myself up into a nice sexual high before the disc jockey interrupted with a few words about the time and weather. I climbed out of the car and used a pay phone to call Judge Garcia.

I reached Patty, Hector's clerk.

"Mr. Montez. Oh, yes, the judge wants your call. I have to get him off the bench. He said to interrupt if you called. Please hang on, okay?" I agreed to wait. A few minutes later, Hector's voice shouted into my ear.

"¡Cabrón! I've been trying to reach you since the funeral. We need to talk, Luis. Can you come over here? I should wrap up this motions hearing right before lunch. Meet me here. It's important, Louie."

"I'll be there. Take it easy."

The phone went dead and I was left trying to figure out what I could do for Hector. If killers were really after him, then he needed protection, and I was no good for that. My botched attempt to rush to Orlie's rescue had amply demonstrated my lightweight ability in that area.

I dropped my father off and drove the few blocks over to the courthouse. Hector was handling the whole thing rather badly, but I shouldn't have been surprised. When we were students, Hector had easily manipulated the symbols of the times. He had problems with any idea of substance. I remember doubting the strength of his principles. I had questions about his inner stamina, his sense of knowing when it was that a line had been crossed and he had to take a stand. His long hair and fringed jacket looked impressive in the newspapers and he was useful as a speaker. The man could rap. He sailed through undergraduate school on scholarships and stayed on the dean's list, although the rest of us skirted with flunking out because of all the meetings, or because we had spent a week camped on the university president's lawn. He knew early on that he was going to apply for law school. He talked me into taking the law-school aptitude test. I was surprised that he had joined the Berets. When I asked him about it, he beat around the bush. Finally, one night over beers at a downtown bar patronized by locals and students looking for color, he told me there was something about the whole military ideal that fascinated him. He dug uniforms and discipline. It had nothing to do with revolutionary fervor for *la raza*. It did not surprise me when he put on the uniform of a judge and meted out discipline in his courtroom.

Security at the courthouse was tight. In addition to the usual metal detectors and inspection of briefcases and purses, cops lined up in the halls, eyeing everyone who passed through. I had to be searched again before I could enter Garcia's courtroom, and I was allowed in only because I was an attorney. More cops sat in the courtroom pews.

Hector saw me and motioned for me to sit in one of the chairs at the front of the courtroom. He was in the middle of a suppression argument earnestly presented by a young public defender who kept hitching up her skirt and clearing her throat. The judge obviously wanted the hearing to end and she was taking too much time. The cops enjoyed the show and didn't bother to hide their lack of respect for the lawyer's argument.

"It is apparent, Your Honor, that not only did Officer Clark not have probable cause for searching Mr. Montoya's automobile, he didn't have probable cause for stopping him. The fruits of that search were tainted early on and cannot now be used. It seems to me that—"

Hector interrupted. "Ms. Bailey. Can you tell me what Officer Clark should have done when he saw the beat-up 1974 Ford in the Cherry Creek neighborhood, moving down the street without lights at three in the morning? And, Ms. Bailey, what should the officer have done when, once he did stop your client's car and asked for I.D., your client failed to produce any, he clearly didn't live in that neighborhood, and he acted intoxicated?"

"Your Honor, excuse me. But there is no evidence that Mr. Montoya was intoxicated or did anything remotely suggesting that he had been drinking. Officer Clark testified he concluded that from the way Mr. Montoya was acting. But there isn't anything to back that up. And what is this about him not living in that neighborhood? All the police officer knew was that he was a Hispanic in an older automobile out late at night. If that's enough to be stopped, then I guess we better tell all the Hispanic residents of Denver that you can't drive at night in any neighborhood except the poorer ones unless you want to be stopped by a Denver cop who will then come into court and say you were acting suspiciously. Is that what this court is going to conclude?"

Hector was too brown to blush, but his eyebrows rolled into one dark line across the bridge of his nose. I knew the public defender had scored a point. Unfortunately, it also meant that the judge was going to nail her client and let the appeals court resolve the issue. It wasn't good strategy to point out to the distinguished judge the perils of ethnic life in the city.

"Ms. Bailey, I'm not sure what I am going to conclude, except that I will take this motion under consideration. Until I issue my order, the bond for your client is continued and I expect that both sides will cooperate in preparing for the trial of this case, which, as I recall, is set for next month? Thank you. That will be all. Court is now adjourned." He ended it so quickly that the cops had to step over themselves as they swarmed to the bench to offer a thin line of protection. Hector waved at me to follow him and then disappeared into his chambers.

The cops let me through, not without some hesitancy. The judge's nervousness had infected his bodyguards. I entered his bright, roomy office, a little uptight myself. The room had always been neat, but now it looked cluttered and dingy.

"This is good, Hector. You going on like this, under the pressure of threats and Tino's killing. Good press. The justice system won't be intimidated into closing down. But you must have every cop in District Two in your courtroom or the hallway. I'm not sure I feel so safe on the streets."

"Come on, Louie. None of this was my idea. I was ready to postpone everything, but that prick Anderson couldn't find a replacement judge to take over my docket. What a useless excuse for a chief judge! Anyway, I'm done. I'm taking off tonight. Replacement or not, this particular judge's duties are finished until somebody figures out what the hell is going on."

What *did* he think was going on? Why, after twenty years, were he and Orlando and Tino targets? It had to be more than a crazy racist finishing up what he started in the middle of mesquite and scrub grass so many years ago that the details were lost forever. But then, crazy racists were capable of doing exactly that.

Patty stuck her head into the office.

"I'm sorry, Judge. But there's an urgent phone

call. A man named Martinez. Says it's life or death. I didn't know what to do, I can take—"

"No. Give me the call. I'll take it here."

The phone buzzed.

"Orlando, this is Hector."

Hector wouldn't look at me while he talked to Orlie. He scribbled notes on a pad and tapped his pen on his desk. He didn't speak. The thick roll of eyebrows reappeared and a line of sweat glistened where his mustache used to be. He hung up, again without a word.

I waited. Hector packed random papers in his briefcase. It was obvious he was stalling. He didn't want to talk about what Orlie had told him.

"That was Orlie. He . . . he got another call. Threatened him, me, my family. I have to go home to make sure Maria and the girls are safe."

"Hold on, Hector. You called me, man. You said you needed to talk. You've been trying for days to see me. Now, suddenly, you have to go. You're worried about your wife and kids? I'm sure they have more cops sitting in your front yard than you do down here in your courtroom. What the hell is this? Level with me, Hector. What's going on?"

Hector made his way to the door of his office. "I'm scared, Louie. That's what it is. I'm afraid. There, I've admitted it. I'm going to hide. This call from Orlie cinched it, that's all. Good-bye, Louie. You should talk to Orlie." And then he waltzed out the door. I ran after him, but the crowd of cops slowed me and the last I saw of Judge Garcia was his back, surrounded by uniforms, as he rushed through an exit used only by judges.

7

I used the clerk's phone to call Teresa, but her secretary said she was in conference. I left my name and a message that I would try later.

The walk across the street to the police station took me about five minutes. It took another ten before Detective Coangelo lumbered up to where I sat in front of his desk, responding to a page that a lawyer wanted to talk with him. He surrounded me with his bulk and shook my hand, his fingers smothering mine.

"Montez. Right? Long time since I've seen you. But the trial was only, what, a week or two ago?"

"Something like that. I should have listened to you. You warned me that Toby would get burned."

"Does me good to see the justice system work, you know what I mean? That old scumbag received his due process, fair trial, the whole nine yards. Now he'll do real hard time. Some guys never learn. He hasn't been sentenced yet, has he?" He wanted to be there when the judge lowered the boom on Arriega's worried gray head.

"No. But that's only a formality."

He sat down and the chair squeaked under his weight. I had heard the department had instituted new physical-fitness requirements, including weight standards for all officers. Apparently, the weight memo hadn't yet made it across the detective's desk.

"You don't want to talk about Arriega. That's old news. What loser are you defending now?"

I ignored the gibe. "I guess I don't know who else to talk to. Not sure you can help. But it's like this. Tino Pacheco's killing, and the threats against Orlie Martinez and Judge Garcia." It wasn't a question, so Coangelo stared at my face as if it were a traffic light and he was waiting for me to turn green. "I've known those men for years. I was here the other day with Martinez. He reported telephone threats and the hassle he's having with Hummy Gonzales."

The cop's eyes lighted up. He would do almost anything to nail Gonzales on something serious. He leaned forward and I heard the wood in his desk cry out for relief. "Okay. So I know all that. We're talking to Gonzales, giving him a little undesirable company, at least from his point of view. But those telephone threats aren't Hummy's style. If he's dealing with a problem, he confronts it head-on. That's why he's done time and that's why he'll do it again."

I was quite familiar with Hummy's direct style of problem solving. "That may be. And yet Judge Garcia is running home as we speak, because he doesn't know what to make of all this, except that Tino Pacheco had his backbone exploded. Orlie Martinez is a wreck, and somehow this has something to do with Rocky Ruiz."

"If you want theories, I have plenty of those. Take your pick. Pacheco's always been on the fringe, shall we say. A couple of his business associates were at the funeral. Bookies making sure that his bad debts really were uncollectible. He owed them plenty. Pacheco liked to show off for some of his tenants. You can drop a bundle at the dog races if you want, and apparently he wanted to plenty of times. So maybe your boy Tino owed too much to the wrong person and they collected in the only way they thought they could. It's been known to happen, counselor."

"If it was gambling debts, they would have roughed up Tino first. Give him a chance to pay up. A shotgun is pretty final, Detective."

"It's a theory. Tino had a reputation for being a tough guy. Maybe someone decided to show him who really was tougher, only they needed a little extra firepower to help make their point."

I shook my head and he knew I wasn't buying it.

"And, of course, there's this Rocky Ruiz killing and the hooded men threats. Between you and me, that one is the fishiest. Only Martinez gets these calls. And the hooded men thing was shaky twenty years ago. Today, it looks like a toothpick house sitting on a bowl of jelly."

And yet that was the official explanation. "The Ruiz killing was political," I said. "There were FBI agents out here, cops from this station, the attorney general's office. Hell, you name the agency. No one turned up anything else. Neither did the grand jury."

"You know how it was, Montez. In those days, we had a damn red squad running around like crazy, dealing with bomb threats, terrorists, student take-overs. They called Denver the bomb capital of the country. Politics was hot, and we were looking for kooks from the Left and the Right. If your friend was killed by men in white hoods, well, it sort of fit into the pattern."

"It was easy to explain, you mean." He shrugged and about a ton of flesh vibrated around his neck.

"Look, Montez. I can't tell you much, number one, because we don't have much and, number two, except for the fact that you knew the victim, you really have no business in this. You're a lawyer, an officer of the court. I'll give you that."

"Thanks, Coangelo. I know that deep inside somewhere you could learn to like me." I didn't elaborate. I didn't want him to think I was dragging his size into the discussion. "Try to understand, Detective. Tino Pacheco was part of my life a long time ago. Maybe it's a Chicano thing—I don't know. It would help me if you told me anything. There's one too many dead friends around and a couple of others who are running for their lives."

"I don't give a damn about no Chicano thing, whatever that is. Leave the detective work to us, Montez." The artificial air in the sterile cubicle had dried up my sinuses. I felt cold. Yellow sweat rings stained Coangelo's shirt. He might have sighed as he started to explain what he thought I should hear. "We have the body, the method, the time and place. That's it. It could be one of several reasons why Pacheco was hit, and it could be something that we haven't stumbled on yet. We're looking in several areas, checking on the backgrounds of people he associated with. Like you, counselor. Seems like I saw a report on you the other day. Some trouble with the supreme court about one of your cases. Is that it? Something like that. You ought to be cleaning up your own backyard instead of whistling in the dark about your murdered buddy. I don't think there's much you can do for him now."

I ended the conversation with a grunt that was supposed to thank him for his time. I wanted to ask what gave him the right to poke around in my affairs? Why did he think it was necessary to dip into my troubles? But then I remembered he was a cop and that was his job—digging through people's trash until he found something that stuck to him other than the smell. Good-bye and good luck, Coangelo.

The fresh air felt good in my lungs after the air-conditioned climate of the police building. I worked up a little sweat on the way to my office and my knees stiffened from the exercise. It was enough to convince me that as soon as I had some time I would drag out my old ten-speed and hit the bike paths. It was an odd thought. I worried about my physical condition while my business fell apart, Tino lay in a freshly dug grave, and I couldn't win a case if I was on the jury.

Those eyes. Teresa was real. I had no idea how I would pull that off, but I promised myself not to dwell on it. Knock on wood, *ese*.

Not much had changed at the office except that I had more desperate messages from clients and Disciplinary Committee lawyers. Nothing new from my father. One of the ex-wives called. And Gregorio Leyba paced nervously in the waiting room. He had decided not to wait until tomorrow to see me. I waved him off, but he caught me before I reached the door to my office.

"Louie! I need to talk with you. I'm running out of time. I need . . ."

"Give me five minutes. I have to make a call. I'll see you in five minutes." I shut the door in his face. I knew things were bad if I would rather talk to my ex than a client. I answered Gloria's call.

"What's up?"

"Bernardo wants to play football for the school. They have a football camp next week that he insists he has to go to if he wants to make the team. They gave him a physical and the school doctor said he might have a heart murmur. He needs a special checkup to play. It's stupid. There's nothing wrong with his heart, but they won't let him practice unless a specialist okays it. Can't you do anything?"

"What does Bernie want to play football for? He's fourteen years old; he looks like ten. They'll kill him out there. Tell him this is high school and he ought to be concentrating on his classes. He's running out of time if he thinks he's going to go to a good college."

"He's only a freshman, Louie. He'll do all right. He's smart, you know that. A little lazy, that's all."

I couldn't imagine where that came from.

"Is this heart thing serious?"

"He had a checkup at the beginning of summer— when you talked him into going out for Little League, or whatever that was. He's in perfect health. It's that old school doctor. A little uptight about potential lawsuits, I guess. You lawyers ruin everything."

"Yeah, sure. Next time you're arrested, call a doctor. So let a specialist examine him. If he wants to break a leg playing football, I guess he'll do it."

Gloria paused. I could see her twisting the telephone cord with her skinny fingers. "The insurance won't cover this specialist. You going to pay for it?"

"Damn it, Gloria! I knew it had to be money. You'd think I'd learn after all these years. But I called you and it never fails—you want more money."

"I can't help it, Louie. I need to pay his tuition at St. Thomas's so he can start classes. Plus about three hundred for books. He needs school clothes, football shoes. I could use some help, Louie."

"My check shows up every month."

"And I spend it every month on him. Look, I don't want to argue with you. I was through arguing with you years ago. Can you do this or not?"

"How much for the specialist?" I had already lost the war. It didn't seem appropriate to fight the battle.

"Who knows? A couple hundred, I guess, maybe three. I'll take him to the doctor, tell them to send the bill to you. Okay?"

"You tell him to call me. I want to talk to him about this football baloney. If he really wants to play, he has to convince me. Three hundred bucks is a lot of money to throw away if he doesn't stick it out. He quit baseball, you know."

"This is different. A lot of his friends are on the team. He thinks he's fast. Talks about catching passes. I'll tell him to call you. Will you be home tonight?"

I hadn't heard from Teresa. "Yes. I'll be there."

Nothing like reaching out and touching someone you once loved, maybe still do, and getting jammed.

72

Hey, the boy might make a good wide receiver. He had speed, good hands. I could do worse than spend my Friday nights or Saturday afternoons trying to spot him with my binoculars out of twenty-two scrambling bodies on a muddy football field.

As soon as I hung up, Evangelina passed through another call. It was Teresa.

"There's a reception sponsored by the firm tonight. Give everyone a chance to meet the new associates. Around six. I need to be there. I want you to go with me, Luis—hold my hand. I hope you can make it."

I hated those things. "How formal is it? I'm wearing my old blue suit. I need a haircut." I can play hard to get as well as the next dumb cluck. If I didn't think about the possibilities the night offered, I might make it. But the perfume I had smelled the first night I met her caught me off guard, over the lousy phone! "Where shall I meet you?"

We arranged the details and I was on my way to expressing something ridiculous when Gregorio knocked on the door. I said good-bye and hollered, "Come in!" I hadn't resented a client this much since my legal-aid days when a divorce case blew up over the weekend and I had to shelter a desperate woman and her three bratty kids until I filed a restraining order on Monday.

"I paid you two grand for my bankruptcy. Where is it? I'm losing money. Customers have heard I'm in trouble. They're holding back, waiting to see what I do. You need to step on it, man."

I grabbed his file out of the filing cabinet and dumped it in his arms. "The papers are in here. Sign them and have Evangelina make copies. I'll file them first thing in the morning." The damn papers cost me most of a weekend. I needed to finish a few details, but Leyba could sign what was needed and maybe then he would be satisfied.

"Is it all here? This is very important to me, Louie. I'm counting on you."

"You want your retainer back? You can hire someone else, if you can find anyone stupid enough to go through your nonexistent books and records. I had to recreate your business history for the past two years, Leyba. I told you it would take time. Now either sign the papers and leave me alone or take back your check and get the hell out of here. I don't have time for this!" A nervous hoarseness had crept into my voice. I wanted to keep cool, try to save whatever attorney-client relationship might remain—I needed that two grand—but it wasn't happening. Leyba stared at the file, shook his head, and was about to walk out.

"Oh, screw it. File it tomorrow, Louie. I'll sign these. Take it easy, hombre." He whistled, then quietly shut the door.

I stood there for a few minutes in the middle of my office, surrounded by file folders, legal pads, telephone messages, law books, and one or two framed papers that showed the world I could engage in the practice of law if I so chose. I looked around the space I had created for my work. I didn't really see anything. The colors, shapes, and textures blended into a hazy, dull blur. I loosened my tie and sat down behind my desk. I wanted to be with Teresa, to dance in a joint packed with Mexican nationals, hollering like a kid with his first paycheck, spinning my beautiful lady around the dance floor, the envy of men wearing boots and fancy western shirts, and I wanted a drink.

I reached for the first folder on my desk, opened it, and tried to remember what it was I was supposed to be doing. I still wanted a drink.

8

$\blacklozenge$

The reception provided a convenient excuse for the firm of Graves, Snider and Trellis to show off: new people, the impressive array of guests who would attend one of its bashes, the fine digs. For the firm, it meant a good party. The thing took place in a cavern with the anomalous title Conference Center. The building that housed my office could fit in the Conference Center and there would be extra room for one or two actual conferences between a few dozen lawyers and their clients. Only the best carpet, wall coverings, furniture, and finger foods. Glass panels covered one entire wall, providing a view of the mountains and city lights that should have inspired the lawyers in the firm who had any sensitivity at all to ask, What the fuck am I doing here?

There were so many lawyers, judges, and politicians that I felt like a delegate at a convention.

A few people of color had made the guest list and I guessed that somebody important had rubbed

Graves, Snider the wrong way about community involvement, a more polite term than affirmative action.

Teresa and I were met head-on by a tall, pale man with wispy hair and bad fingernails. I liked him, though. His suit was in worse shape than mine.

He kissed Teresa on the cheek and hugged her shoulders. She turned to me and said, "Luis, meet Tom Robinson, coordinator of the firm's pro bono programs. Tom, this is Luis Montez." She wiggled out of his grasp. It figured that he would be in charge of the free work for poor people.

He pumped my hand energetically. Flakes of dandruff rolled down his shoulders.

"Hello, hello. Pleasure to meet you. Haven't we met? The bar's Committee on Legal Services, maybe?"

"I don't think so. I'm not much of a committee man. Maybe in court, on a case?"

His face wrinkled and it was obvious that he didn't know what to do with a lawyer who didn't belong to committees.

"I doubt it. My job here is to line up firm attorneys with cases referred from the legal-aid office, when they have a conflict, or no one available, or the case is out of their expertise. But I don't really do many cases myself anymore. Administration, you know."

After he duly impressed us with a quick rundown of the firm's many projects and commitments to pro bono work, Mr. Robinson wandered off. I grabbed Teresa's arm and pressed my lips to her ear. "Did I tell you I don't like to do this?" I wanted to kiss her.

"Only about a dozen times since you picked me

up. I don't like it, either. But you know as well as I do that I have to be here—for a while, anyway. We'll leave as soon as we can. I promise."

One of the minorities approached and I prepared for the worst. Thankfully, it was Flo from the radio station. She acted as relieved as I to see a recognizable face.

I pecked her on the cheek, then hugged her. Teresa stood back about a foot and I made sure she saw the *abrazo*. Kissy, kissy at these things.

"What are you doing here, Louie? I didn't think this was your style."

"My friend here works for the firm. And, shazam, here I am. You know how it is."

Flo looked Teresa over and chuckled. "Yeah, I know how it is." She introduced herself to Teresa and made the obligatory small talk. "Too bad you don't want to help sponsor an hour or two of music. Maybe the Mexican show on Sunday morning?"

"I'm not sure I'll have the rent, Flo. I'm afraid I'm a lost cause as far as your station goes."

She accepted that. "If I'm going to hit up any of these big-time lawyers for underwriting, I better move it. So far, the only guy I've managed to corner was a tall, weird person with no sense of humor." Before she walked away, she grabbed my arm and said, "I heard about Tino. And that it goes back to Rocky. Be careful, Louie. Call me if you need something." Then she floated into the crowd.

I survived the evening by adding Teresa's share of drinks to mine. She didn't want to loosen any office gossip, so she stayed with club soda. I ordered gin and tonic from one of the wandering waiters, a drink

I seldom try, and learned I liked it. There are times when I order a drink off the top of my head, usually when I'm not paying for it, and I tend to overdo that type of drink that night. I also tend to suffer the next day with symptoms I'm not prepared for, like pain in the back of the head or behind my nose.

A group of men and women in one corner caught my attention. I knew most of them weren't lawyers. I recognized a few, by name anyway, and I was intrigued by their presence.

"What are Ray Candelaria, Bruce Thompson, and Fay Arguello doing here? They may have a few bucks, but this is a little odd for them. Somebody running for office?"

Teresa surveyed the group. "Those are the firm's newest clients, Luis. The baseball stadium thing. They represent a group of investors who want to build the stadium near downtown. We're helping them lay out a package, line up the support in the city government, do the paperwork needed by the major leagues, details like that."

I remembered as soon as she said it that they had all been mentioned in the newspaper article. They must have been busy. The minority investors group, using somebody else's money, had finagled an in with one of the most powerful law firms in the city.

"Are you working on that?"

"No. I'm just sort of here. Since I'm not licensed yet, I have limited responsibilities. I may do some research down the line. A lawyer named Terry Sheehan is their main person with the firm. He's the guy in the middle with the gray hair. But there will be a good group handling their business. Personally, I can't think of anything more boring than baseball."

I immediately thought of dozens of things more boring than baseball—cocktail parties, for example. But that discussion was for later. I was curious and had enough of a buzz that I decided to find out more about the investors. I left Teresa talking with a pipsqueak judge, grabbed another drink, and made my approach.

They saw me coming and exchanged whatever information they had on me. It couldn't have been much.

Ray Candelaria smiled broadly and grabbed me around the shoulders. "Montez. *¿Qué tal? ¿Cómo estás?* You know everybody, no? Folks, Luis Montez. A lawyer, what else?" He laughed and the group smiled as one. I shook hands all around.

"I'm surprised to see you here, Ray. I guess now that you've drifted into professional sports, you need to hang out with a different crowd, eh? More variety than the usual union convention, no doubt." Candelaria worked with labor unions. He could be a business agent one week and a consultant the next. His real income came from a string of liquor stores he owned with a variety of partners. I had always admired his ability to balance the two identities with what appeared to be a minimum of effort.

"You know how it is, Luis. We're serious about this stadium proposal. It will do wonders for the community. The construction alone will provide hundreds of jobs for guys from the Westside." I failed to understand how unemployed, untrained dropouts and Mexicans without papers would land jobs with construction companies that had their own crews, usually nonunion. It might have been one of those details that would be taken care of in the proposal. Later, much later.

Candelaria droned on. "Once the team is here, think of the opportunities. Restaurants, bars, hotels. The cab companies. I'm excited. Maybe you're interested in joining us. We're always looking for new investors, Luis."

"I like baseball. As a spectator. That's about it. I'll take a couple of season tickets, though, if you can fix me up."

Fay Arguello, whom I didn't know, laughed. "You'd be surprised how many people ask us for tickets. We've a long way to go. We're only now starting on a plan with our lawyer. But if you want to play, I would encourage you to do it quickly."

Candelaria followed up. "That's right, Luis. Talk to some of your associates who want in with us. We've figured out some interesting concepts. Anybody can be an investor these days."

Does that include a down-and-out Chicano lawyer in a worn suit and a glazed look in his eyes from one too many gin and tonics?

"People I know are investing with you? Like who?"

The three of them talked at once. The general drift was that names were confidential. I could understand that, no? But people I knew quite well wanted in. Ask around.

You bet. I'll ask my secretary and my father. Maybe they had committed their life savings to a scheme to sell off the land and homes of Westside families for the great sport of baseball. Between them, they could probably come up with five hundred bucks.

I told myself I was interested because I loved baseball. The truth was that I wanted to know what they were up to. I had enough curiosity to mix it up with people I normally crossed the street to avoid. I drew out a few more platitudes from Ray about the great opportunities. Then I tried to be a little more specific. "The city has its own land for a stadium. You must have a good inexpensive proposal if you expect to have a chance. You have to keep costs down. Way down, I would imagine."

Candelaria was into it. He liked talking about deals. "We proposed a site near the major streets leading into the city. More than adequate space for parking. Close to the downtown mall and the Civic Center. For a damn good price. The city has to listen to us; we're too competitive to be ignored. Man, we got it covered."

"Yeah. I thought you would, Ray. The story I read said you think the stadium should be built near the junkyards and warehouses next to the Westside. That land should be cheap." Candelaria, Arguello, and Thompson stood in a neat row, one continuous smile connecting them, their dark faces shining in the glow of the expensive indirect lighting. I killed off my drink. "But how about the people? What happens to the dozens of families who live around there? Some of them are my clients. They've lived there for years, can't afford anything else, don't want to live anywhere else. What do you intend to do with the people you'll have to move?"

Sheehan stared at me. It was his turn. "The Candelaria stadium proposal is way ahead of you, Mr. Montez. The plan includes adequate compensation for homeowners and businesses. Quite fair, actually."

"But it can't be too expensive, or the city won't listen to you. You buying new houses for these people? You including moving expenses? You prepared to find replacement housing nearby so that kids don't have to change schools? There's an elementary school down there. What happens to it? And if a little old lady doesn't want to go, won't sell for any price, does your plan include lawyer fees for the court order you're going to have to serve on her?"

Sheehan's attention was riveted on me. "Your concerns are noble, Mr. Montez. However, I think you're getting a little carried away. No one will be forced out. We have the utmost confidence that once people hear the offers we are prepared to make for their land, homes, or businesses, there will be no problems."

Ray needed to say something. "That's right. We did a study, Luis." A rain storm crossed Sheehan's face, but Candelaria didn't notice. "A damn poll. Those people out there will sell. They don't care, man. *No hay chiste.* And there's not going to be any."

The smiles had disappeared. I started to back away from the group. "Well, I guess I don't have as much faith in a survey as you do, Ray. I can't begin to imagine who from this firm would go down there to ask questions for a poll. But it must have been in Spanish, right? And the illiterates had it explained in detail? But then, this is your deal, not mine. I'm sure your lawyer has given you the best possible advice your money can buy. Somebody's money, anyway."

Terry Sheehan cleared his throat. He turned to the group and started giving instructions. "Montez raises interesting points. We'll talk about them again sometime. But there are a few people I want you to meet across the room." He looked over his shoulder at me. "Please excuse us, Mr. Montez."

I eased away and found Teresa.

"Is it time yet? Because if it's not, you may have to find a ride home. If I stay much longer, I'm going to do something that might cost you a very promising future with these freaks."

Those eyes. They laughed at me, then melted my resentment of the party, then coaxed me to lighten up. When she had me, she said, "Let's go, Luis. You're right. You and I need to talk, anyway."

She had moved from the Corsican Plaza into a very comfortable town house near Sloan Lake—quiet, reserved, professional. Wood, chrome, and glass surrounded the stiff black furniture. Her bedroom was in a loft at the back. We had a drink.

She said, "Tell me about the judge and Martinez. What is all this? What happened to Tino?"

"I think the accepted version is that he was in with the wrong people. Gambling, maybe drugs."

"I can believe it. Tino was a bimbo, Luis, a player. He knew plenty of strange characters. I met some of them. They could have killed him that night."

"A bimbo is one thing, Teresa. A victim is something else. Not my image of Tino. I thought you liked him. You were pretty cozy the night I met you."

"We knew each other. We were pals, I guess."

"Pals?" That wasn't the right word.

She gave me the funny look I deserved. "Friends, Luis. I never slept with him."

"I didn't mean anything. I don't want to lay any trip on you. There's no reason."

"That's right. There's no reason for you to ask. I think I expected more."

I remembered the kiss from the night of Tino's funeral. "Teresa, I'm not good at this. I don't know how to say what I feel. But you must see that you mean something to me. Something special."

"You're crazy, man. Don't do this. Don't start about my meaning something to you, Luis. I'm not ready for that. I don't want that. Whatever you do, don't make this more complicated than it already is."

She had her plans. There was no room in them for me. I was an accident along the way, and I believed right then that the whole thing between us would be over soon enough and that she was absolutely right. I didn't need another relationship to go bad. There were obvious limits on what we could mean to each other. And I knew it and I felt it and I could almost taste it, and when I kissed her I thought, Damn it, I need you, Teresa, and why can't I tell you?

She walked away.

I thought her face glowed. I should have said, Tell me what you want, let me try, give me anything.

She said, "I want to be your friend, Luis. I like you.

85

You're the one decent person I've met here." I smiled and shook my head. I didn't want to be a decent person. "Don't laugh at me. Maybe you can't understand. What I need more than anything right now is a friend, that's all. Is that too much?"

"It might be, Teresa. I haven't been anyone's friend since Rocky. I'm not sure I remember what it means."

"What is it with you guys? Why is it so hard for you to deal with a woman the way she wants it? Does it always have to be your way?"

"It's not that, Teresa. I think every man has his own idea about somebody he wants to end up with. Women must think the same way. We all want the dream. Most of the time, we end up with something less. Time runs out or the options aren't there. I've had my fantasy. God knows, I've tried to find it. Somebody I can talk to without feeling self-conscious. A strong person who doesn't really need me, I guess. A contradiction. Someone independent enough to say she wants me the way I am."

"And off you go, into a little blue heaven?"

I was stiff and uncomfortable and she wasn't making it easier on me. "Call it what you want. You wanted to know why men want it their way. I think we all do, men and women."

"Tell me, Luis. This Earth Mother fantasy—have you ever come close?"

I plowed into it. I didn't think about what she would think tomorrow or what I might be giving up. "There was a lady once. Didn't stay with her long. She ended up married to Rocky, my best friend. We managed to fight about her one night. He knocked the crap out of me. But for a time, we had something. Her name was Margarita."

Whatever spell I had cast with my bumbling attempt to be sincere passed with the clink of ice in her empty glass. The eyes that changed with the light turned away from me, inward, and I knew it was time for me to go.

"I want to call you, Teresa, see you again. I think we can like each other, if we give it a chance."

"Maybe, Luis. I'll let you know."

And for the second time a good night and a goodbye were all I coaxed out of her. The summer finally had worn out. A breeze whipped the well-manicured bushes along the walk from her door to the street. I buttoned my coat and rolled my shoulders forward in a feeble effort to hang on to a bit of the warmth of the past few weeks. A light, cool rain started to fall during the ride home. The rhythmic knock of the windshield wipers almost smothered the music from my car's radio. I had a hard time falling asleep.

9

──────────◆──────────

The football player had called. "Dad. It's your son. I need a physical to play football. I'm going tomorrow. I'll call after. Thanks." No, son, thank *you*.

Only one other message. What had happened to Orlie and Hector? A few days ago, I couldn't avoid them, and now—silence. Maybe they had finally calmed down.

Jacob Abrams had left the second message. The attorney for the Disciplinary Committee sounded as if he was about to lose his professional decorum. "Mr. Montez. You can't avoid me much longer. If you don't meet with me, I'll have no choice but to commence formal proceedings against you. Gaston Peters filed a complaint and you need to do something about it. Call me tomorrow."

Why were assholes ready to investigate the little guy at the drop of hat? A hardworking sole practitioner who didn't have the resources of one of the firms to back him up shouldn't have to respond to an investigation started by a minor complaint. It wasn't as if Peters had been hurt. Hey, he'd won the damn case. The lawyers who worked every hour they could squeeze out of a day, on the brink of bankruptcy, fighting it out in courtrooms every week—the trenches—not hiding behind the paper blanket of insurance work, commercial transactions, tax or real estate—we were the ones the Disciplinary Committee went after with a vengeance. Throw in the fact that I had a certain ethnicity and good old boy Abrams had to be drooling at the prospect of nailing my hide to the wall behind the bench of the supreme court.

I tried to reach Orlie at his house. No answer. I took the long way to my office, about ten miles long to be exact, and stopped at Hector's house in Park Hill. The wide tree-lined streets were quiet. The leaves had started to turn. Pockets of rain splashed on my car as I tried to find space along the curb. Except for policemen camped in a late-model blue van, there was no hint of trouble in the neighborhood selected by one of the morning dailies as the best part of town to live in before launching a political campaign.

The cops were on me as soon as I parked.

It didn't take long to convince them that I was harmless. They checked with Maria before they allowed me to knock on her door.

The pale ghost of Hector's wife opened the door. She hugged me, her body shaking slightly. She clung to me for a few minutes, then ushered me into the large living room. Photographs of their children hung on every wall. The judge had often said his family was his first priority.

Maria sat down on the couch after she poured me a cup of coffee. I remained standing.

"I came by to see if Hector needs help. The last time I saw him he was so uptight, he couldn't talk."

"He's not here, Luis. He's been gone since last night. I don't know. . . . I can't think. . . ." She stopped talking. She stared at the wall and made no attempt to continue the conversation.

"What do you mean, Maria? Where did he go? What's he doing?"

She started to cry. "Luis, I'm so frightened. He's been acting strange, scared. We sent the girls to my mother's. We were going to leave. Stay at the ranch for a while, until we knew what was going on. And then, last night."

The woman kept drifting off. She didn't want to think what I was thinking. She didn't want to remember Tino. "What happened last night?"

"He had some calls. One from Orlie. He was shouting with Orlie, really arguing about what they were going to do. At least it sounded like that's what it was about. He wouldn't talk to me about it. He said he had to see Orlie. He said he would probably stop by your place. I guess you didn't see him?"

"No. I got home late. There wasn't any message from him." The tears rolled down her face. I handed her my handkerchief. "When did he leave? Didn't the police go with him?"

"Around midnight, I guess. I thought the police were with him. But this morning, they told me that Hector insisted on going alone." She broke down completely. "Oh, Luis. I don't know why he would do

90

that! Where is he? What's happened? What am I going to do?"

"He left as soon as he talked to Orlie?"

"No. There was another call, a little later. Hector was on his way out. I didn't want him to go. We were fighting. I was afraid. I pleaded with him not to go, but he insisted. Then the phone rang. It was a woman. She apologized for calling so late. She asked for Hector. He didn't say anything. He just listened. He wouldn't tell me anything about it. He left right after that call."

"And you haven't seen him since?"

"No. I wish he would call. He knows how crazy this is making me. Why doesn't he call, Luis?"

I had no answer for Maria. None of this made any sense to me. "He didn't say who the woman was?"

"Someone from the courthouse, worried about him. I didn't believe him. But I don't know what to think."

In my clumsy way, I tried to comfort her. I assured her that it would be all right. Hector was probably with Orlie and they were figuring out what to do. He was a judge, he knew people, and he was taking care of this. She had to try to relax. She would be okay as long as the police were around. She had to make sure they knew Hector was missing. She thanked me for trying to help.

"Do you know who the woman could be, Luis? If you do, you have to tell me. I can't take not knowing. I don't care who it was. I don't think it would matter if it was . . ." She left it unsaid.

That thought had never occurred to me. Maria and

Hector had a marriage that seemed to work. But then, what was working? "Don't worry about that, Maria. For as long as I've known Hector, he's never been the kind of guy to play around. You and the kids are the most important things in his life. You know that. If Hector said it was someone from the courthouse, then I'm sure it was. Maybe Patty or . . ."

"I know Patty. I'd recognize her voice. It wasn't her. Hector said her name when he picked up the phone. He called her Teresa. And that's all I heard him say."

I called Abrams as soon as I reached my office. He wanted to see me that minute, in his office, immediately. I told him I would make it over later in the afternoon. He wouldn't accept that. "You're going to regret your uncooperative attitude, Montez." I had regretted it all my life, but there it was, so what could I do?

"In case you don't realize it, I need to make a living. I can't rearrange appointments and deadlines to talk to you simply because another lawyer says I'm unethical."

"I've tried for days to set something up with you. If you don't deal with this, you may not have a living to make, at least not in law." He let that sink in. "Look, Montez. I have my own deadline. The full committee meets this afternoon. They want my report. I will tell them you ignored this whole thing and that will seal it, Montez. After that, your next chance to talk will be when you testify at the formal hearing. If you want to avoid that, you better talk to me. As soon as possible."

There's always a white guy ready to bust you.

Can't escape them. "Okay. Okay. I'll be over. Give me a half hour."

I managed to tie up a few loose ends on a couple of files, turned over a dozen details to Evangelina, and introduced myself to Abrams's secretary about an hour later.

I knew I was in for a humiliating experience as soon as I walked into his elegant, imposing office. He had degrees from Georgetown and Harvard. A half a dozen photographs captured his kids on the campuses of the best schools on the East Coast. It wasn't difficult to conclude that his idea of fun was a few drinks at the club with supreme court justices, fellow partners from the biggest firms, and a handful of well-heeled clients.

I tried to deal with it, but I had never resolved my basic dislike for lawyers. There was no way I was going to change my attitude for the man who could cut my career in two with the wrong recommendation to his committee.

He went right to the point. "Gaston Peters's complaint is that you and your client physically assaulted him and his client in the courtroom, and that you also ridiculed the judge. Martin Grant hasn't filed any complaint against you, and I guess he won't. He'd just as soon forget the whole affair. Peters, on the other hand, has been very insistent."

"He's trying to build a case for damages. He knows my client doesn't have anything, so he's trying to drag me into this. What he doesn't know is that I don't have anything, either. He's probably better off if he sues Donna Armstrong. At least she receives monthly child-support checks."

"Peters hasn't said anything about litigation. But that is beside the point. Disrupting a courtroom, assaulting a colleague and his client. Closing down the courthouse? These can be serious, Montez."

"Peters wants to sue. He said as much that day Mrs. Armstrong made her point. If that's what this is all about, tell him to call me. I think I can convince him that I don't have a damn thing he could possibly want, including money."

Abrams's face turned sour. If I was telling the truth, he didn't want to know it. "I'm not Gaston Peters's lawyer. I'm not talking to you to negotiate a settlement. I am investigating a formal complaint lodged with the supreme court concerning an alleged breach of the code of ethics and your professional obligations as an officer of the court. If you can't understand that . . ."

"I understand you very well, Abrams. And I am telling you that this is a farce. If anything, I prevented Peters from ending up really hurt. I should have decked him myself. He had a skewed outlook about the case from the beginning. Lawyers like him usually do. They're not used to dealing with people like Mrs. Armstrong, or me, for that matter. He wanted her out of the house in a matter of hours. He was willing to do whatever he could to see to it that she was evicted. That included telling me before the trial that we should settle."

"What is wrong with that?"

"Usually nothing. I've dealt with landlord attorneys for years, and most of them want to settle on the courthouse steps. You'd be surprised how reasonable they can act when they realize the tenant is serious about having a trial. But Peters wanted to sweeten the deal. Insurance, I guess, is the way he looked at it. He made it clear that if we settled and I could convince Mrs. Armstrong to leave immediately, he'd make sure the settlement included a tidy little sum designated as fees for me." Abrams rubbed his hand over his graying temples. "I think Peters was trying to create a conflict between me and my client. He wanted me to sell her out for a couple hundred bucks. In my book, that's a violation of your goddamned code of ethics. What do you think, counselor?" Abrams didn't answer. "But you know what, Abrams? That kind of stuff has happened ever since I entered this profession of yours, and I don't give a damn anymore."

Abrams tossed his pen on his desk pad. He closed my file. "You're a disgrace. Lawyers like you have ruined the practice of law in this state. You don't know the law. You have no respect for the judicial system. You slide through law school and cut corners to make a buck. You represent cold-blooded hoodlums and welfare cheats. And now you're in trouble, Mr. Montez. You better find yourself a lawyer."

Abrams walked around his desk and reached for my arm to usher me out of his office. I jerked away, but he tried again. He said, "Time for you to go, mister." His hand closed around my arm and dragged me to his door.

When I was a kid and I walked away from fights because I thought they were nonsense, my adult behavior haunted me for days. I carried the burden of what I thought was weakness. Later, there were nights with Tino when I had no choice, he made it for me, and we had to fight our way out of bars or parties, and sometimes we didn't make it. And then my recklessness haunted me for days. I used to think, When will I grow up?

Abrams's face was inches away. I smelled cologne, breath mints, and Harvard. I heard Tino. "It ain't no big thing, *ese.*" I slugged Abrams with all the frustration I could pump into my fist. He fell and the blood immediately rolled out of his nose and down across his tie. That was a shame. I liked his tie.

I walked out of the office, expecting somebody to stop me, to arrest me, to wake me up, to tell me, "Wise out, man." But nobody did, and by the time I reached the ground floor of Abrams's building I felt pretty good. Nothing was going to happen. At least not right then. I waltzed through the revolving doors. And that's when the jabbing pain in my ribs twisted me in two. I banged into a wall and tripped onto the sidewalk. The punch I threw hurt me much more than the supreme court's investigator. When would I grow up?

10

I rested for a few minutes. The mall was packed with office workers taking their noon walk. I weaved through the rush in the general direction of the offices of Graves, Snider and Trellis. The day was overcast, but I had to loosen my tie. My skin felt hot and clammy. If I bent my body at the hips and leaned sideways, my ribs didn't ache as much as when I tried to walk upright. I must have looked like Charlie Chaplin, waddling down the street, except old Charlie never exhibited the same contorted facial expression. Secretaries and bankers strolled by without noticing that I almost passed out each time they bumped into me. The two blocks took me twenty minutes.

I eased out of the elevator on the twenty-ninth floor. The reception area spread out for miles. At any other time, I would have marveled at the panorama of mountains that greeted all visitors to the wonderland of Graves, Snider. Under other circumstances, I might have flirted with the smiling young woman sitting behind a desk and a complex set of telephones. Another day and I might have been impressed with the layout.

All I could think about was that Teresa made much more money than I did even though she had graduated from law school less than six months ago. The firm knew how to attract talent.

My tie lay at an awkward angle across my chest. Tiny drops of sweat rolled off my chin. The young woman stared at me for a minute. If receptionists could talk, what stories they would tell. She coughed and said, "Can I help you?"

"Ms. Fuentes, please."

"Do you have an appointment, sir?" She picked up a receiver, ready to connect with somebody.

"No appointment. I need to see her."

She started to punch in a number, then remembered something. "I'm sorry, sir. But Ms. Fuentes isn't here right now. Do you want to leave a message?"

"When will she be back?" I leaned against the counter. My breathing came in short bursts of air I expelled like a locomotive. The girl looked very worried.

"I can't say for sure, sir. Maybe somebody else can help you?"

"No thanks." I felt an attack of vertigo coming on. I turned to leave, but I didn't make it. My feet fell out from under me and I pitched forward, right into the meaty arms of Detective Philip Coangelo.

I must have been out for a few minutes. I lay on a large, soft couch in what looked like a lawyer's office. Coangelo stood over me and behind him was a harried, nervous Tom Robinson. I recognized the large white flakes plastered on the shoulders of Robinson's dumpy suit.

The lawyer peeked over the policeman's head. "Is he going to be all right? We should call a doctor, I guess."

Coangelo didn't look at the pro bono coordinator. "Yeah, I suppose you should. I'll keep an eye on Mr. Montez." Robinson took his cue and left.

I tried to sit up, but somebody had jabbed a railroad spike through my lungs and I was stuck to the couch. "I think I finished cracking my ribs."

"Must have been when you slugged Jacob Abrams. His nose is broken. He wants you arrested. Thought you lawyers resolved conflict in the courtroom? Isn't that the general idea?"

I didn't think I should talk about Abrams. "What are you doing here? You're not here for me."

"I think we're looking for the same person. I wanted to talk with your friend Teresa Fuentes. You may have heard that she's not around. I, uh, looked over her office and was leaving when I saw you take your dive. You almost landed on one of the expensive-looking vases these guys keep around to impress clients." He pulled out a pack of gum. His pudgy fingers labored over the wrapper, but finally he slipped a stick into his mouth. "What was it you needed to see Ms. Fuentes about? Looking for a good lawyer? You may need one if what Abrams reported is anywhere near right."

"Thanks for the help, Detective. My visit here was personal. Why are you interested in Teresa?"

"You better watch these social calls. You don't seem to handle disappointment very well."

I didn't respond. Breathing was increasingly much more difficult and I hoped that Robinson knew how to use the phone. Coangelo pushed a chair next to the couch and sat beside me. I was in the shadow of his bulk. His face turned into a massive hunk of flesh staring into my eyes.

"I told you we were checking out the people who kept company with Tino Pacheco. Interesting assortment of characters. There's you, of course. You have your problems, but nothing like Tino. Gamblers, druggies. Generic hoodlums. Lots of young women. I'm surprised he found time to collect rent. And then there's Ms. Fuentes. Really out of place in Tino's life, yet there she was. Looks like they were pretty close, too." I didn't want to hear any of this. "So we sniffed around. Not only her. She turned out to be the most intriguing. In fact, we couldn't really find out much about her. Traced her back to law school, then college, and that was it, for a while."

"What do you mean? I don't understand." I wheezed and coughed.

"Take it easy, Montez. You're going to pass out again." I closed my eyes and listened to the detective. "She didn't exist before college. At least Teresa Fuentes didn't." A red haze flashed through my eyelids. "I hate computers. You know what I mean? Everything's run by the damn things. Can't do any police work without knowing how to call up a data base or word-process a memo. And they can be a real invasion of privacy. But you'd be surprised what we can learn from them. You should look up your file one of these days, counselor." I nodded my head. You bet, Coangelo. "The court records from

Texas are in miserable shape. What do you expect? That's Texas." I nodded again, to be sociable. "We figured it out, though. It got easier once we learned she was from Brownsville. A name change and, bingo, a brand-new person. I needed to talk to her after I saw that court order giving her a different identity. Claimed it had been her name for years, so she made it legal. And then this thing with Tino, and the telephone threats. It started to make a little bit of sense. Couldn't figure you out. What the hell did you have to do with it? But now I think you were one of those innocent third parties we read about in the papers." He stood up and the floor creaked. "She's gone now. And I guess you don't know where she is. Wouldn't be here fainting if you did. If you see her, tell her I sure would like to talk to her. I'm real interested in what she knows about what happened twenty years ago. I'd like to talk to her about the murder of her father. And why she came all the way up here to hang around with the guys who were with Rocky Ruiz the night he was killed. I'd really like to talk to her about the way Tino Pacheco died. I'm sure you can understand, counselor, that I am very interested in that."

Maybe it was my ribs. Maybe it was the cryptic message in the detective's words. Maybe it was a little bit of everything I had stumbled around the past weeks. Whatever it was, it finally did me in. The red behind my eyelids throbbed against my eyeballs at a steady, painful rate. I heard the pounding deep in my eardrums. I felt Coangelo sit on my chest, slowly, so slowly. He crushed his weight into my body and pushed me through the couch. The floor cried for pity until it gave way. I dropped twenty-nine stories to the street. As the crowded mall rushed up to grab me, I wanted, needed to scream for help. I wanted to scream.

PART TWO

◆

But I'd lose them all
Burn em all
Go along without all of it
Give up the chances I see
If you'd raise me up
Take me up
Let me know the heart of it
Give me your sweet soul dream.
—Karl Wallinger, World Party

My body was in shambles. My business in worse shape. My license to practice law was about to be yanked. I spent a couple of days in the hospital before I walked out with bottles of pain tablets, stiff bandages for my ribs, and a numb, blunt smoothness wrapped around conclusions I didn't want to make. I received, by certified mail, two demand letters from lawyers threatening to sue me for injuries to Gaston Peters and Jacob Abrams. Old man Leyba called Evangelina and let her know I finally was fired. He wanted his money. I couldn't find Hector or Orlie. Tino was dead. One of my children needed to have his heart checked out just to play football.

And Teresa, like summer, had slipped away in the rapidly cooling mountain air.

I did the only thing that made sense. I caught a plane to Texas and checked into the Al-Re-Ho Motel in Brownsville.

11

I needed a few more days of heat. My body wanted the warmth of the sun and my head craved clear, dry air to clean out the fog.

I'm not sure what I expected. Cowboys and Indians? Certainly not palm trees and a pounding ocean surf. But Brownsville offered all that and more. The humid coastal air removed any lingering thoughts of the approaching Denver winter.

I had food delivered to the motel. I found beer and newspapers at a gas station. The pain in my body stayed with me like the steady, monotonous beat of the drummer in a Mexican wedding band. I swallowed tablets of oxycodone with the beer until the bottle was empty, then I turned to aspirin. A radio blared Tex-Mex music. Dust swirled against the windows. The sound of the changing season kept me awake the first night. Sleep drifted in and out with vapors of muggy air. I lay on the narrow bed and hoped the healing process would work on me.

The ceiling of Unit 8 had thirty-six cracks, two

cobwebs, and one glob of something brown. The room's color scheme reminded me of the blur from a roller coaster roaring above a nighttime amusement park.

I couldn't remember leaving the city. A few phone calls to Evangelina, my father, and Gloria, and I neatly clipped the ragged edges of my life. My secretary knew where I was, my father understood I would be gone for who knows how long, and my ex-wife accepted my apology for not talking with Bernardo. The specialist wanted to run a few more tests on the boy, just in case. Gloria assured me she would explain to my oldest son that I had to be away on business. My exit wasn't graceful, but it worked.

The morning found me groggy and stale. I read through the phone book. Fuentes, Ruiz. Plenty of relatives but no Teresa. I asked the motel's manager for phone books from the nearby towns and he brought me a few—San Benito, Harlingen. Again no luck.

I called information and asked for Teresa Fuentes. "Sorry, sir, I have no listing under that name. I have a Cleofas Fuentes, Isidro, and a Margarita. Actually, there're quite a few. But Teresa or the letter *T* doesn't show up."

"Give me the number for Margarita. And her address, too, please."

I once fought over a Margarita Fuentes, suffered a black eye, and almost lost my best friend. I once made love to a Margarita Fuentes. And her eyes, passed on to her daughter, had hinted at passion in the bright fluorescent lights of Lolly's Taco Shack, creating an unanswered promise that pulled me from my urban shelter to the flat, edgeless world of the Rio Grande valley.

Margarita lived in San Benito, about twenty minutes from Brownsville. I didn't bother to call her. I finished off a warm beer, showered, and shaved. I climbed into a pair of jeans, old boots, and a new cotton shirt I had thrown in my suitcase with its straight pins and cardboard inserts. The shirt covered a second, half-empty bottle of yellow tablets meant to soothe my burning ribs. I had a few for breakfast.

It took several tries before I arranged a ride. The green and yellow cab pulled up to the wooden steps that led into my room. The driver was a young Chicano with very long hair who listened to country music. The handmade sign attached with tape to the back of his seat announced that his name was Ricardo Sanchez and his automobile was the Gran Sol Taxi Cab Company.

"*At your service, sir,*" he said to me in Spanish. "*You're lucky to find me. I am the most reliable, the most able cabdriver in Texas. And the only one you can find today. Where may I have the honor of driving you?*"

I was embarrassed by my weak Spanish, but I tried to answer him in the tongue that should have been native for both of us. "*San Benito. Here's the address.*"

He looked at my note and nodded his head to the beat of somebody wailing about the "last time, baby." "*I can take you there, but it's out of town. Be ten or twelve bucks.*" He started singing along with the radio, translating the hokey lyrics of the Nashville superstars into beautiful Spanish poetry of love, pain, and struggle.

We sped past houses snug against one another, lawns green and roses in bloom. I counted a dozen bars packed with men before we left the city limits. Ricardo drove along Elizabeth Street and kept following it after it turned into State Highway 415. He found an exit for the interstate, obeyed the signs that pointed to Harlingen and San Benito, and we were off into the horizon. The prairie rolled up to greet us as soon as the last house faded into a dim spot. Texas surrounded us, Ricardo lapsed into silence, and the only sound came from the radio.

I had filled the summer before my final year at the university with bits and pieces of drama and romance. Rocky, Orlie, Tino, I, and a handful of other Third World college students, mightily trying to grow up, rushed through those few months from meetings to foreign movies to poetry readings to early-morning revelry at the reservoir, all against a lush green background of homegrown marijuana and a gray haze of alcohol. Our hair hung across our shoulders and some of us had patches of flowery cloth sewn into our jeans. We joked that it was the last chance for the children in us to live. For Rocky, it was his last summer.

Margarita carried the feel of her homeland. Tan and lanky, a country girl who wanted to be an artist, she surprised the Chicanos on campus who assumed she would fall for their macho city jive. She quickly, and quietly, informed the men that she had no time for their youthful endeavors, and yet she assumed the role of guardian for us all, the person who made sure we had a place to sleep if we were too loaded to make it home or who provided a bowl of beans from the pot she always seemed to have simmering on her stove.

Rocky brought her with him from Texas. The mother of his young daughter, she was a few years older than Rocky. They tried to find her niche on the campus. She developed her own friends, art students mainly, and she had little to do with his political activities. She worked in town and took care of their daughter and some of Rocky's friends who managed to fit into her life.

I bobbed and weaved for her attention, never formally announcing my combat with Rocky, doing what I could to impress her with what I thought she would find important.

I paid for part of my education by working as a tutor with the university's minority-recruitment program. A small number of incoming first-year students lived in a dormitory preparing for the grind that faced them in the fall. A group of the older students tried to train them—how to study, make outlines, set priorities. They were high school kids and we were the college assholes who did what we could to intimidate them. I'm afraid we didn't do much for their college achievement.

I had asked for Margarita's help with some of the women who were feeling especially homesick. They were young girls from strict, traditional families who lived in the San Luis valley. I had no idea how to reassure them, how to convince them that they really did need to attend this college, where they would be totally out of place, surrounded by strange, alien people who spent more on clothes than their parents would have for food all year. Margarita did a good job, but in the end the students admired her more for her role as wife and mother than as a liberated woman. Margarita, after all, was not a student.

The campus buildings dwarfed us as we made our way through the Quad after her session with them. I felt invisible in the shadows cast by the century-old trees and the moon.

She continued a conversation we had started weeks before. "I don't know if I'm coming back. It's hard on me and Victoria and Rocky. We never have money. He's so busy, we hardly see each other. Back home, I can live with my mom and dad, work in town. My mother begs me to take Victoria back. Down there, I could try to do something of my own. Here, there's no chance."

"You have a job. Your artwork. What's all that?"

"It's part of this, Luis." She pointed at the trees and buildings. "It's not me. Rocky needs this. He likes this. It's like Victoria and I are in the way. It would be easier on all of us if we were gone."

"I don't think it would be so good on Rocky. He loves you and Victoria. He needs you."

She stopped walking and turned to me. "I love Rocky, too. That's not it. He has what he needs right now. I need something else. I don't know if it's back home, but I have to find out."

"It'll be tough on a lot of us if you leave. Who will take care of us?" We laughed. I grabbed her hand and held it in both of mine. I rubbed the skin of her knuckles. "Rocky's a lucky man. I wish I'd known you before him. I should have visited Texas long before Rocky took me down there. I should have met you years ago."

"Rocky and I were kids when we were married. We still are, Luis. I had the baby, we got married, we moved up here. It was as fast as that. I don't know what's going on anymore."

My hands jumped from her fingers to her hair. I stroked her face. We kissed and held each other, more from relief than anything else.

I said, "I'll miss you. More than Rocky will. At least he has his time with you. I squeeze in a few minutes here and there. I make up reasons to drop by your place, to see you at the damn library. I don't want you to go."

She didn't answer. I felt a shudder run through her. She pressed against me, kissing my face. We lost ourselves in an embrace, the fresh night air heightening our senses until we were overcome and we let our youth justify our lovemaking.

"What was the number again?" the cabdriver asked me in Spanish. *"These San Benito streets are crazy."* I handed Ricardo my note of the address. *"Yes. Over by the park. No problem, guy."*

We passed a group of white buildings fenced in by chain link topped with barbed wire. The yard was filled with people standing in tight knots. A public-address system blared across the camp. Ricardo turned up his radio to drown out the noise of the refugee shelter. Hundreds of people waited for some-body to make a decision about their immigration status. I saw a boy near the fence, the same age as Bernardo. He stared at the cab as we drove by, dust from the cab's wake floating over him, settling in the compound.

The house sat back from the street, a wide expanse of grass surrounding it. It was a gray stucco place with a station wagon and a beat-up truck parked in a red rock driveway.

A pair of black dogs ambled up to me as I paid Ricardo and asked him to wait for a few minutes. I didn't know whether Margarita was home—hell, I didn't know whether this was where she lived.

The dogs jogged beside me, escorts to the front door. They were comfortable around visitors.

There was an instant then when it finally hit me. Texas. A woman I hadn't seen in more than two decades. The fantasy I had created about her daughter. And the death of a friend of both of us, killed in the same manner as her husband. Suddenly, Texas was too small for this visit and I was too old to confront the past.

She opened the screen door.

"Luis. I wasn't sure you would come. It seemed like you should. I've been waiting."

She had kept her lanky beauty. A streak of gray ran through her brown hair and her arms and neck were a few pounds heavier. The impression she made was more like a sunburned cowgirl than a *tejana* from the Rio Grande valley.

"Maybe you can tell me what it is I'm doing. You always knew before I did." The dogs ran around me as I stood on the walk. I looked back at Ricardo and waved him away. He honked his horn and drove off. "I assume it's okay for me to stay. He's the only cabdriver for miles, he says."

Her face broke into the smile I remembered. "I told you I've been waiting, Luis. I expect you to stay." We hugged and I held her close again, different people embarrassed by the passage of years and events, not sure of what it was we thought we shared.

The house was a studio for her art. Half-finished paintings rested against the walls. A pottery wheel took up an entire corner of the large front room. Rags, brushes, and painting supplies cluttered the floor and the wooden shelves she had hung along the walls.

"I guess you found your place. You make a living doing this?"

"Of course not! All this is what I do when I can't avoid it, when I have no excuse to postpone it. I'm a teacher. For years, ever since I earned my degree. About five years after I left Colorado. This is a hobby. It takes up the rest of my time."

We were having a difficult time talking. I wandered around the house looking at her work. She manipulated strange combinations of materials to create montages and three-dimensional pieces. Copper wire, marbles, plastic beads. She fashioned mobiles out of spark-plug wires and hung ceramic animal statues on the ends, faces from newspaper photographs glued to the heads. It was all very frenetic, very busy.

"You want coffee or a beer?"

"A beer. Why not?"

She brought one from her refrigerator and invited me to sit at her kitchen table, the only piece of furniture not swamped with her hobby.

"Okay, Luis. We can study each other now. Tell each other what we think."

"Go right ahead, Margarita. I'm not that brave."

A wide toothy smile parted her lips. "Margarita. Nobody calls me that anymore. I'm Rita, or Mrs. Calderon. Margarita sounds so old-fashioned."

"Calderon?"

"My last husband. Long gone. The second one after Rocky. I never worked up enough enthusiasm to change my name. My students were used to it, so I kept it."

"Where does Fuentes fit in?"

"I used it when I first came back. I . . . I guess I was afraid after what happened to Rocky. I dropped Ruiz, never went back to it. Why do you ask?"

I was asking about Teresa, but I told her something else. "The phone company had you listed as Fuentes. It was the only clue I had about where to find you."

"Fuentes is what I have everything listed under. I never changed anything. Around here, everybody knows everybody else; names don't matter. The phone book, the utility company, insurance papers—all under Fuentes. But I've been a Gonzales as well as a Calderon. I assumed you knew where I would be. Guess I thought you would know how to find Teresa."

I spoke too quickly. "Where is she?"

"She's . . . around, Luis. She told me about you, Tino, Hector, and Orlie. It was amazing. All of you in one place. And there she was, in the middle."

Her tone deepened; the words came out faster as

she talked about her daughter. A pink flush crept up her cheek. In the fading afternoon light, she cajoled visions from her memory about us and her child, Rocky, and old friends, and it was no longer important that I was there. We reminisced for several minutes.

"I look back and it's like it never happened. The only real memory I have of Rocky is Teresa. Seeing you again, Luis, it's like a dream. A part of my life that I didn't understand then and I can only dimly remember now. You all seemed so alive then, so young, I guess. And I could only watch it. Rocky and I knew that. I was leaving when he died. We talked about seeing each other in Texas. But neither one of us believed it."

"Rocky loved you and Victoria. You know that."

"It wasn't enough. I don't know what is. Teresa blamed me, I think, in some way for Rocky's death. No, not his death. For him not being around. Somehow, that was my fault. She never understood her father's killing. Who could? She was only four years old. She was mixed up, always in trouble. It became worse as she grew up. She started calling herself Teresa, and dropped Victoria. I ran her out of my house when she was a teenager. She was mean, hateful, always lashing out at me or somebody else who tried to be close to her. She lived with a man until he finally had enough and threw her out. I took her back in because I had no choice. It was rough on both of us. I forced her back to school. Kept at her to do what she needed."

"That's hard to believe. The Teresa I know is in total control. You see what she is now, Margarita. You did a good job."

"I don't take the credit, Luis. She was turned around by her father, by Rocky. He's the one who made Teresa grow up."

She pushed away from the table, walked to a wooden counter covered with jars of ground chile, black pepper, and garlic. She opened one of the drawers and pulled out a leather portfolio battered and torn with age. I recognized it immediately. Rocky had carried it with him wherever he went. He scribbled in notebooks and on pieces of paper that he carelessly stuffed into the case. A frayed brown ribbon halfheartedly attempted to keep out prying eyes.

"Teresa read through Rocky's papers. She had so many questions about those years that I couldn't, or wouldn't, answer. I guess she found what she needed in there."

"You've never read his stuff?"

"I can't, Luis. I've tried. I don't make it very far. Whatever's in there, it's for his daughter, and you, I guess. There's nothing left for Rocky to say to me."

"Margarita, I know this is weird, strange. The craziness in Denver. The police want to talk to Teresa about Tino." I paused. "And I simply want to talk to her."

"You will, Luis. You made an impression. You're under her skin, you damn old man." Her smile returned and it was obvious that my place in her life was not as important as I thought it had been. "She'll be by later tonight. You can stay here, or she can call you. I think she wants you to read this." She handed me Rocky's papers.

12

◆

Rocky's history of the movement, meticulously memorialized by him to help maintain equilibrium in the heady days of youthful revolution, lay before me in a composite of yellowed paper and faded photographs. Newspaper clippings were mixed in with his poetry. I didn't know where to start. I picked out a thin spiral notebook and read.

NOTE FROM MIDNIGHT

A natural gift
This pen from you
Creates colored stones
Among sand
Pushed along the beach.

Always you.

Scribbles offer
Amazing insight
Celebrated conflict
Ideas sure to
Melt the sun.

Always you.
Chapter 8
The Great Chicano Novel
Edited, now familiar
The ink dries
Pause and wonder.
Always you.

Margarita had given Rocky a fountain pen for his birthday. It was a distinguished gift, black with gold trim. He loved to use it, to write furiously in his notebooks. He had it with him constantly and we got used to the ink stains on the front of his shirts.

I read more pages.

It was a damn good time for growing up.

In the dormitory room, the night's litter of beer cans and empty cigarette packs trickled from the narrow closet. The smell of marijuana sweetly hugged the air. Eight young men sat on the floor against the wall. The talk was fast and loose. The men bragged about the movement, dissected the music, basked in the pride created by their involvement in the events that were changing the world. Chicano rock and roll bounced against the walls. At four in the morning they celebrated the demonstration.

Jimmy's head filled with acts of revolution, heroic battles of the Chicano people, and the changes that had to happen, that were happening while they gathered for the party that, in its own way, also symbolized the movement, the revolutionary protocol.

"This is our chance; we have to make things happen. Tear away a piece of this country and use it for what we want. A new Aztlán, the rebirth of Chicano culture, music and art. Our own leaders and schools. As long as we don't jack it up, as long as we stand our ground and take it. Like our black brothers, we have to seize the time!"

All but one in the group shouted, "Right on!"

The man who did not join in the political cheerleading was short and dark, with ringlets of kinky hair across his forehead. He drank pills with his beer, his skin glistened with sweat and his red-rimmed eyes stared from a bronze, pockmarked face. He wore jeans and a jean jacket. Political buttons hung on his shirt and a small red star on the front of his dusty, oily stevedore's cap bounced the light. He had arrived on campus the week before the demonstration. He badgered students with his discourses on the revolution, the coming wind of change that would roar over the bourgeois state, and the need for armed struggle. He was animated with emotion when Jimmy saw him. His hands waved rapidly, emphasizing his words, and his enthusiasm flowed over his listeners, infecting them with idealistic energy.

"I work full-time for the revolution," he would say. "This is my job—no pay—no vacations—no health benefits. I work for the people."

Jimmy dragged him into the talk. "Oye,

118

Carlos. What did you think of today? Righteous, no?"

Carlos shrugged. One hand rested in his jacket. He spoke, slowly. "It reminds me of the beginning of the Frisco State strike. At first nobody knew what to do, but the more we dug into it, the more we learned from experience and so we caught on. There were Panthers, S.D.S. We took on the pigs every day for weeks and by the end some genuine revolutionary effort had taken place. We kicked some pig ass. That may happen here, quién sabe? It will take a while for this movement to mature."

"Cut us some slack, bro." A hint of a challenge lay under the surface of Jimmy's words. "Dudes here have done as much as anybody in the country. The Chicano Movement is a reality. We're moving and we'll do what we have to, when we have to. I don't think we have to explain ourselves to you. Who are you anyway, man?"

Carlos smiled. His eyelids quivered, then drooped over his eyes, and he studied the young men in the room. "I work full-time for the revolution, ese, and I'm telling you, you all have a ways to go. It's been happening all over the country, and you think you discovered something new. In East Los, the Chicanos have gone beyond this lightweight student power trip and real revolutionaries are working with the gangs and hypes, to turn them from counterrevolutionary lumpen elements to shock troops of the vanguard. You all don't even know what that means, yet."

He drank his beer. "Don't take me wrong. With some organizing, some leadership and the correct political line, this hassle here could get down to basics, to power for the people and the genuine war we all will have to fight one day." He finished the can of beer, then tossed it on the pile of empties. Quickly, he opened another.

Jimmy said, "You're too much, man. You don't know what you're talking about, nobody understands you. You try to give that political rap to the brothers on the Westside and they'll kick your ass just to pass the time. You might need it, too. Nothing I know about you says you're not a pig, man." Jimmy raised himself from the floor and grabbed a beer of his own from the six-pack on the table. He lit a cigarette and leaned against the wall.

Carlos wiped his forehead with a large flowing red bandanna. "¡Pendejo! I ain't no fuckin' pig. But what I see around me are a bunch of middle-class, would-be movement heavies, more interested with their newspaper clippings than with the people. That's all I've seen these past few days. Políticos with a mediocre rap, trying to act like they know how to do the thing, but nobody's convinced me. I ain't seen no soul, no commitment. You all have time to do. You see, I been where

you're at now. I know where you're going. I've
seen it in Frisco, Madison, L.A., New York.
You don't have it yet, some of you never will.
Some of you will be swept away. Like the
Chairman says, away with all pests." He
laughed and the men were insulted more by
his laughter than his words.

Jimmy rushed to the shorter man, his steps
quick and light like a boxer. "I've had it, man.
You shut up, or I'll take you out." He grabbed
the collar of Carlos's jacket.

Carlos rolled to his side and whipped his
hand out of his pocket. It held a small black
pistol. He waved the gun in Jimmy's face.
Jimmy stopped, frozen by the weapon and
the cold, desperate look in Carlos's eyes.

"Don't touch me, pinche. I'll do you in so
fast you won't know it 'till you drop." As he
clawed his way to his feet, he pointed the gun
at the men in the room, including them in his
threat. He locked the door to the room and
motioned with the gun for everyone to slide to
the far wall. He ordered them to huddle
against the closet door.

"Now you'll learn about revolution." His
sharp laughter echoed against the music. He
finished his beer and threw the empty can at
Jimmy. It bounced off Jimmy's chest.

"Talk about chickenshit. The way you tried
to jump me. I don't have time to waste with
you small-time punks. I have things to do."
He walked around the room looking for another beer. He called the men sellouts. He

talked of bombs and shootings. He said he would die fighting the pigs.

Jimmy leaned against the wall, unable to act, not understanding what Carlos was doing. He thought of the night his father shot their sick dog, and he remembered the blood and gore and the tiny whimper from the dog as it died.

Carlos searched his jacket for the bottle, poured the pills on the table and scooped one in his mouth. There seemed to be more people in the room than when this had started.

Jimmy said, "Look, man, the sun's coming up. Let's cool it and . . ."

"Shut up!" Carlos lunged but Jimmy reacted immediately and knocked him down. He jerked the gun and it fired. The shot dropped the men to their knees as the bullet knocked a hole in a wall. Carlos crawled on the floor under a hail of punches and kicks. Jimmy wrenched the gun free and pointed it at the head of Carlos. Carlos stiffened and waited for Jimmy to do something. The young men looked at each other, then at Carlos, then at the gun in Jimmy's hand. The sun broke through the curtains on the windows and the room turned white with light.

I didn't remember the incident described in Rocky's story. It might have happened.

There were other poems and stories. I doubted that any of them had been Teresa's catalyst. I leafed through more pages, not sure what message from

Rocky I expected, not sure I could find the answers that had apparently come to Teresa.

The love for life I saw in Rocky's writings almost embarrassed me. The people he met, the ebb and flow of the tide of change he thought he was living through, the spectrum of noise, emotion, and tension—it all thrilled him, drove him forward. He lived for the fight for justice and equality—words that I had a difficult time saying, that sounded weak against the background of twenty years. Rocky believed the words. He was a martyr, long before he bled to death in the prairie darkness. He suffered in ways none of us suspected. He paid with his wife and daughter, his youth, eventually his life. He might have been the only person I knew who carried the movement in his soul, who wore it like an invisible coat, who basked and gloried in it without expecting a payoff.

I found a picture from the campus newspaper—Rocky, Orlie, and I, arms around our shoulders, fists clenched in power salutes. Three kids with political buttons covering our shirts, ragged hair and headbands proclaiming rejection of whatever it was anybody else stood for. Toothy smiles reflected our victory. MATHEWS ACCEPTS UMAS PROPOSAL—MINORITY RECRUITMENT BEGINS THIS SUMMER! That was Rocky's proposal. He designed it, convinced the administration, and directed it when it finally was in place. The recruitment program was the high point for us. It was the last time the three of us were so close.

March 8. The meeting was a disaster. Paranoia runs rampant. We need a lesson in revolutionary discipline. Orlie and Tino were at it again. Demanding more aggressive tactics. Orlie sounded ridiculous when he quoted Mao. "Power comes out of the barrel of a gun." What in the hell does he think we will do? Hold up a bank? Burn down the adminis- tration building? What we really need is some time with los parientes, remember what the hell this is all about. Hector was stoned again. The guy is useless when he's like that. Orlie insists we need him. Why? We argued late into the early morning and I dragged my- self home, to find Margarita up with Victoria, who had been sick for most of the night. It was a bad night all around.

I pulled out more of Rocky's handwritten notes and passed over his stories and poems. Sandwiched be- tween the attempts at literature and art was a record of the last year of his life, a record of the movement that finally killed him.

March 22. I've about had it. The guys are so uptight, too tense. Mathews won't meet to talk about the demand for a separate degree in Ethnic Studies. The people from Denver sent a message that it was up to us to make a play. They will support us, come to the campus if we do something "dramatic." They want us to do the dirty work, end up arrested and thrown out of school, then they will climb on board the bandwagon. Orlie was all for it. Tino, too, of course. It's out of hand.

April 5. Finally. A project we can sink our teeth into. The Unity Conference. UMAS bought into the idea, agreed to try for funding from the student government. Building a foundation for Aztlán. I feel invigorated, reborn. But still problems at home. Margarita and I talked and I think it is better if she goes back to Texas, at least for a few months. We decided to go ahead with the plan we've kicked around for almost a year. I want to work it out but I can't focus. I owe her so much more and I can't seem to do it.

April 11. Orlie continues to push for "revolutionary action." He's convinced Tino and Hector that we have to pull something off during the Conference, when the campus is packed with activists. Too many of us to single anyone out—they won't be able to see the forest for the trees—that's the line. I wish I could talk to Luis, but I don't know where he's really at. He parties too much, enjoys being a Chicano playboy. But he doesn't take Orlie seriously and that helps put things into perspective. The one constant is Victoria, although Margarita has drifted away. She's a beautiful child and so aware. Every father must think his daughter is the perfect child. If only I could be the perfect father.

April 14. A few more weeks for the Conference. Cinco de Mayo. The university is paying for it! Cultural Awareness Week! I love it. The

UMAS people have put their hearts and souls into this project. They've taken care of the publicity, letting all the groups know about it, lining up speakers. Tijerina will speak on opening night. I plan to help with the session on writing the Conference Plan, our strategy for taking the movement the next step forward. I'm working on it already. Even the Gorillas have taken time out from their revolutionary ivory towers and pitched in. Man, something's bugging me. "If I really bug you baby, then you don't love me."

The balance of Rocky's notes consisted mainly of scribbles about the final days of setting up the conference. That time was hectic. Almost five hundred people showed up from around the Southwest, mainly because Reis Tijerina's appearance added a certain legitimacy. Rocky was so wrapped up, I rarely saw him, and I was busy, too, working with groups of students arranging rooms, transportation, meals, microphones. The few minutes with him were rushed and frenzied. We gulped diet pills and vitamin C to ward off the evil flu bug that ran through the student ranks, laying a few flat on their backs. Rocky looked worried and I assumed he feared for the success of the conference. The fact that it deteriorated into an ugly internecine argument must have been a hard blow.

May 3. Have to reason with Tino. He can't do it. He must know about Orlie.

13

I stopped reading, my eyes strained from deciphering Rocky's small, precise script. Texas darkness covered the world. Margarita had left. "Going to walk the dogs." I had trouble accepting what she had become, but there was no reason for it. What had I expected? A mourning widow, grieving twenty years after the death of her husband? Or the young woman I had loved, carrying a torch that only I could extinguish? It bothered me that she received my ghostly presence without dragging up the impassioned night in the middle of the campus when I tried to convince her to leave Rocky.

I found another beer in her refrigerator. I had finished off a six-pack. Weariness crawled over me and the soreness in my ribs flared up into a dull ache. I played around with the option of calling the Gran Sol Taxi Cab Company. Maybe spend one more night at Al-Re-Ho and map out a plan for dealing with the chaos back home.

I knew I wouldn't leave until I had talked with Teresa.

I pushed aside plates and bowls and laid my head on the table. My eyes spasmodically closed and jerked open as I struggled against losing whatever hold I still had on consciousness. I felt the heavy air wrap around the house. Dogs barked. Margarita's wild mobiles twisted in the space above her sad, colorful paintings.

I watched myself crawl to the door. The eternally playing radio from the motel appeared on the porch. Static and buzzes. A long silence. Furtively, almost unnoticed, music entered the house. The harmony of a guitar, fiddle and accordion created a tune I thought I recognized. An old man's voice sang plaintive words about the heroism of my slain friend. "El Corrido de Rocky Ruiz" glorified the brave and impetuous Rocky who sacrificed everything for his friends and his people. The ballad crept under the screen door and filled the house with courage, pride and death.

I rolled my head on the table, unable to sit up. I thought I must be asleep.

Inmates from the immigration camp danced on the lawn. Stern, rigid men in straw sombreros silently twirled heavyset women wearing dresses sewn in Columbia, Nicaragua, and El Salvador. My cheek turned numb where it rested against the wooden slats of the table.

Teresa made her way through the crowd of children and dogs. Her long red dress flowed backward with the breeze. The screen door creaked and she walked in, her eyes hidden by shadows cast by the flying art pieces.

I couldn't speak. She helped me out of my shirt.

Her hands floated across my chest and I felt the ridges in her fingers and the delicate touch of her palms. The pain in my ribs disappeared. I followed her into the bedroom and watched while she undressed on the edge of the bed. She spoke in Spanish and amused me with jokes about Texas.

An earthy and ancient song composed by her Indian ancestors surrounded us. Smells from centuries ago when we embraced on grass mats in the heat of a tropical night perfumed our bodies. At last, I could see her eyes. They pulled me into the vulnerable space she protected, and when I was there I knew I could have whatever I wanted and I wanted her.

Margarita shook me awake. I was on her couch, covered with an old *chorongo*. "You want some breakfast? We were about to eat." I raised my head and saw her and Teresa near the table where I had passed out. Steam rose from cups of coffee.

"What a fucking headache. I think I picked up the flu, something. I didn't hear you come back."

Margarita stared at Teresa. "I know. You were asleep on the table when we came in. We didn't want to wake you. I found your empty bottle of painkillers. Are you trying to finish yourself off?"

"They're for my ribs. I banged them up a little. I must have overdone it. I'm sorry. I didn't want to be any trouble."

Teresa shook her head. "You look bad, Montez. I thought you were frazzled in Denver. Somebody has to take care of you because you're not doing a good job of it."

"I'm willing to let you try. It might be more than you can handle."

She made her way to the couch. She pushed away my feet and sat on the cushions. "What are you doing here? You came all this way for what? To read my father's papers? To find my mother? Whatever you say, don't say it was for me. Don't say that, Luis."

"It was for you, Teresa."

"Damn." She edged closer and kissed me. Her eyes glowed, convincing me she knew a secret I had to learn. I hugged her and pulled her close.

Margarita said, "This is one of the crazier things I've been into in a long time. I think I better go. I need to prepare for tomorrow's classes, anyway." She walked out and called for the dogs to follow her.

Teresa whispered in my ear. "You're a fool, Luis. I'm a fool. I didn't want this to happen. There's no room for this."

"I've heard this before. Don't repeat it. I'm here. You're here. What else is there?"

I reached for her, but she spun away. She turned on a radio. She danced around the room, smiling, mouthing the words of a lovesick *norteño* accordion player. The music was familiar, the scene branded into my mind by the dream a few hours before.

She led me from the couch into a spare room used by Margarita for guests. The beautiful lawyer who turned heads on the Sixteenth Street mall became, in the hazy morning light, inches from my face, a surreal object, enraptured with the physical act of making love. I saw plateaus and corners on her face normally hidden in the city. Her lips melted around mine. And for a few hours, I forgot about lawyers and clients and Mrs. Armstrong and the tormented, beleaguered Orlie Martinez.

"I read my father's words, but I wasn't satisfied. The world he wrote about was alien to me. A movie, unreal. I had to talk to people who knew him. I had to make it come alive. I found Hector, then Tino, then you. You all helped make my father a person, not somebody in a picture I took out of my mother's scrapbook."

"You didn't tell anybody who you are. I watched you grow up for a couple of years, Teresa. You had no right to keep that from us, from me."

"I had every right. There was no need. I read his journal and it was like he was talking to me. Those pages were his diary, the only connection I had with my father. I went to law school because he said he wanted to be a lawyer. He knew he wouldn't do it. He blamed his grades, but there's more in his words. He didn't expect much, like he knew he wasn't going to live to be an old man."

"Rocky never acted fatalistic. He threw himself into whatever he did. He kept all of us going."

"I know he did. That's what Tino said about him. Hector, too. You guys can't help but talk about him. You act like you don't want to, but each of you did, and without any probing from me."

"We couldn't live up to him when he was alive. His death sealed it. We could never reach his level." I craved a cigarette. "You left without telling me or anyone else that you were leaving. The police want to talk to you about Tino. Why you hid your identity.

Why you disappeared after his death. What you have to do with the threats on Orlie and Hector." I told myself I shouldn't do it, but I slipped away from her, put some distance between us.

"If they want me, they know where I am. I'm not that hard to find. You did it." Actually, she had found me. "If you need an explanation, I can give you one." I didn't say anything. "Fuentes is my legal name. I changed it because that's what my mother has used since she came back to Texas." I imagined the taste of tobacco on my tongue. I hadn't smoked in years, but this conversation brought back the hunger. "I was finished, so I left Denver. I found out all I could about Rocky. The job at the firm didn't seem so important after that. I didn't tell you—I should have, I guess, but it would have meant doing all this explaining. I wasn't ready for it. Now I am." I looked around the room for telltale signs that Margarita stashed smokes somewhere in the house. Nothing. "And I didn't tell anyone I was Rocky's daughter because I wanted to hear the truth about him, unvarnished and clean."

"There's more."

She inched closer to me. She kissed me and her lips were cold. I remembered her at Tino's funeral—beautiful, calm, quietly in command. Now, with me, she was beautiful, calm, in command.

"My father's writing told me something was going on with all of you. Particularly with the Berets. Something was wrong. He knew it. He wanted to stop it, prevent it. I don't know what it was. I didn't find out in Denver."

"It could have been that thing Orlie and Tino were

planning for the conference. Their 'revolutionary action.' Rocky argued against it."

"You remember that? He talked to you about it?"

"No. It's in his notes. You read it the same as I did."

"It was impossible for me to know what it was."

She kissed me. My skin shivered. I wanted to feel her heat again, to sense the blood pumping through her in passion and love. But the questions that had been with me since Coangelo told me she was Rocky's daughter wouldn't wait.

"Did you see enough to think Tino and the others had something to do with his death? Did you see enough to carry out your own retribution?"

The silence lasted only a few seconds, the time between the opening and closing of the valves in my heart, the time needed for dust from the ceiling to float down and settle on our blankets: an eternity.

"No, Luis. I didn't see that. If I had, I don't know what I might have done. It's impossible for me to imagine that Tino or Hector or you had anything to do with what happened to Rocky. I didn't avenge my father. I met you. I fell in love with you. And now I don't know what I'm going to do."

I knew. I pulled her a bit closer, covered her with kisses and caresses, listened to the ancient Indian song that hovered over us, and loved her until we finally fell asleep.

Teresa stayed at her grandfather's house, an isolated, weather-beaten ranch. She told me it was cold and drafty in the winter. It featured peeled paint and a broken gate across the front walk. There was no phone. A radio constantly played Mexican music. A dusty television set occasionally flickered in the dark.

Santiago Ruiz scurried in the background, a skinny brown shadow, bent with age and arthritis, not always recognizing his granddaughter. He called me Ruben. Teresa took care of him, temporarily relieving his children from the duty they accepted with grace and pride.

The walls had photographs of stoic young men and women, many in uniforms, staring into the camera on days they later recalled as some of the most important of their lives. A gray varnish of dust covered the oval gold and black frames. Crossed American and Mexican flags hailed the mixture of cultures above the stern faces of heroes and casualties.

I checked out of the Al-Re-Ho and moved my one suitcase into Teresa's bedroom in the attic of the old house. She said it had been Rocky's room.

The old man kept a few animals on his ranch, not of much use, old friends and companions. We rode a pair of horses in the mornings along dirt roads and paths, avoiding fences and gates, staying away from people. My legs and back ached from the rides and Teresa rubbed my muscles and bones, thawing out the early-morning chill, bringing back the warmth of the Texas *llano*. We shared late breakfasts of beans, eggs, and blood sausage with Santiago, captivated by his long, rambling stories about his wife, brothers, children, and Pancho Villa. I rehabilitated my lumbering Spanish and relearned how to converse in my father's language.

I abandoned my pain and exhaustion. I walked

miles around the ranch, kicking at dirt clods, inspecting mesquite and cactus, spying on insects and snakes. I found a break in a fence and spent hours repairing it—hammering, sawing, measuring. I offered to paint an old shed, but Teresa stopped me, laughing at my ambition.

And we filled afternoons and nights, and hours we snatched away whenever we could, in each other's arms, making love, ignoring any other time except the minute we were in. Her smell and taste soaked into my skin, under my fingernails and the rim of my mouth.

We talked about everything except what we should have. She was convinced that she would not return to Denver, but anything more than that was unknown. She had a feel for the law that I envied, and I assumed she would continue as a lawyer, somewhere in Texas. There was no mention of her returning with me.

After a few days, I wanted to show off. I called the Gran Sol Taxi Cab Company on Margarita's phone and convinced Ricardo that he should pick us up, although the ranch was a dozen miles out of town. Teresa thought my extravagance was foolish, almost arrogant in the small town of San Benito, more so because Margarita had plenty of automobiles for us to use. We showered together, washed away the day's worth of dirt and sweat, and readied Santiago for a visit with one of his daughters.

Sanchez, the cabdriver, couldn't believe I was hanging around.

"What is it, man?" he said to me in Spanish. *"I thought you were here like on business, you know, a*

quick trip, then back you go. Denver, no? But, here you are. Turning into a campesino, brother. Better watch yourself."

He overlooked our groping in the backseat of his cab as he drove us into Brownsville.

The Compadre Bar offered beer and a pool table. Dozens of men loitered in the smoky light, talking loudly and profanely about the day's work, the turn in the weather, and the Dallas Cowboys. Many of them vigorously argued local politics. Who ran for mayor and county commissioner apparently was decided by such diverse considerations as unpaid bills, fights from ten years ago, and the respect shown certain elders. A few women wandered among the men, but they seemed out of place.

Teresa and I squeezed into a tiny booth graciously given up by a pair of fat laborers in boots and western hats.

She fit into the booth as easily as she had found peace in the desolate arroyos and scrub brush of the Valley. The bar gave her a certain comfort. "Santiago used to drink here. He'd drag me and some of my younger aunts and uncles down here on Saturday afternoon and we usually ended up taking care of him. I learned how to drive taking him home at night when he was too drunk to handle his old jalopy. This is the closest thing to a hot spot around here."

The men tipped their hats in her direction, asked about her *abuelito*. She was polite and reserved and introduced me to each one who came over to speak to her. I was uncomfortable, not sure how these people would take to a city boy escorting one of their beautiful young women. Other than an occasional smirk, they had no immediate reaction to me. In the background, questioning glances and puzzled frowns came at us from men who cautiously watched me romance their friend's granddaughter.

Coangelo's pudgy fingers tapped a rhythmic beat on the table top. He wanted our attention. "Mr. Montez. Why did I think you might be down here? A little vacation perhaps?" His eyes turned to Teresa. "That wasn't very nice of you to run out on me, after our little talk. I thought I could trust an officer of the court. You'd think I'd know better after all these years."

His body cut off any exit from the booth. Near the door, two local sheriff's deputies nervously stood at attention, watching Coangelo's broad backside. I imagined he had more support outside. "Is there something I can help you with, Detective?"

"Are you her lawyer, Montez? If not, then I'd rather not talk to you. I'd hate to think you aided and abetted a fugitive."

"What are you talking about?"

Teresa touched my hand. "Easy, Luis. He wants to take me back to Denver. For questioning. I think that's the phrase. Regarding Tino. It's all right. I'll go with him. You talk to Margarita and my grandfather. Tell them I had to go back to the city for a few more days. You can help me clear it up."

I stood up in the booth and my legs jammed against the table, leaving me unable to walk. "You must be crazy, Coangelo. She couldn't have had anything to do with Tino's killing. You can't be serious."

The policeman's face was very red. He shouted at

me, inches away from my ears, loud enough for the crowd in the bar to hear. The customers were very interested in the conversation. They stood around watching the only white man in the place harangue Ms. Fuentes and her boyfriend. "You keep popping up, Montez. And you have no business in this. I told you we had the body and the method. The rest of the pieces fell in place when we found out she was Ruiz's daughter and that there was a very good chance she thought Tino had something to do with his murder. Even you should be able to see the connection, counselor!"

He grabbed Teresa by the elbow and tried to lead her to the door. She twisted free. "You don't have to do that! I'll go with you without any trouble." Instead of taking it easy, he produced a pair of handcuffs and roughly snapped her wrist. The men in the bar reacted as if one, shifting their weight from one leg to another, grumbling about the *gabacho*'s lack of respect.

"I think you better put these on. I don't like the odds."

She stepped back from Coangelo. The deputies started toward her, but part of the crowd cut them off. Teresa's eyes glared at the policeman. Rocky's steadiness reached out from within her. "I said I would go with you. Stop the rough stuff."

The huge man stretched his body in her direction. "I don't have time for this. You stubborn bitch, put the goddamn cuffs on!"

Teresa slapped him. His jowls shook and the redness flooded over his ears.

I worked myself loose from the booth and reached

for the detective. Before I could do anything else, the crowd of men surrounded the cop and Teresa.

"Let me through. ¡Por favor! ¡Déjame pasar! Let me by!" The surging mob trapped me. I was dragged and pushed. I couldn't see Teresa or Coangelo. Bodies swayed back and forth, shifting for advantage and space. I heard thuds and a noise like a bag of cement dropped a hundred feet onto the hardwood floor. Men shouted. A shot rang out over our heads and a woman screamed. I flowed away from Teresa like a piece of driftwood in a river, turning and falling, unable to direct my feet or arms. Men in cowboy hats and scruffy boots, hugging bottles of beer, ran as one and carried me to the door. Dark, husky workers with full mustaches and embroidered western shirts surrounded me. The river parted and the men rushed through the street, leaving me on the sidewalk.

It took a few minutes for me to convince myself that I should go back into the bar. The deputies were gone. Coangelo lay on the floor, unconscious. His weight settled and spread out over sawdust and dirt. The jukebox continued to play. Unfinished bottles of beer stood on the bar next to lighted cigarettes. No one else was in sight.

14

♦

"**I**'ve already told you. I didn't see her leave. I don't know where she is. Your deputies grew up around here. If they can't tell you where she is, what makes you think I can?"

"They haven't been sleeping with her, Montez. You know damn well where she would go. You know who took her away. Everybody in this hick town knows. Nobody will say a fucking thing to me!"

I tried not to stare at the huge purple knot in the center of his forehead—a token of the town's appreciation for the good work done by one of Denver's finest. "You're not surprised by that, are you?"

"I'm surprised how quickly you're willing to forget who the hell you are. This isn't going to help your problems with the bar association."

"I guess you don't understand. I don't know where she is. You've checked out the ranch, scared old man Ruiz half to death. You harassed her mother. Now you threaten me. Get this right. I have no idea where in the hell she is, and there isn't anything I can help you with."

We were in the county jail, where Coangelo decided I should sit for a few hours after Teresa had slipped through his fingers. He couldn't hold me for anything, but he wanted assurance that Teresa hadn't told me the address of her hiding place. He didn't know what else to do.

He walked around the cramped interrogation room. The two of us were crowded into the space with a table and a couple of chairs. "Maybe you don't know what's been happening in Denver. Hidden away with a woman like Fuentes, it must be easy to forget your priorities, your values."

"What could you know about my priorities and values? You amaze me, Coangelo. You talk like that and yet if you hadn't tried to muscle Teresa, you'd probably be on a plane with her now, your catch in the bag, ready to turn her over to the DA. You bungled it, Detective."

He wrinkled his face and a maze of lines and creases covered his recognition of the truth in my words. "We all have our days, counselor. I'll find her. Sooner or later."

I wasted one more day in Texas. Margarita insisted she didn't know where Teresa had fled. I believed her. She was worried about her daughter, not because she had disappeared but because of Coangelo's insinuations. Teresa's knowledge of her father's youth should have been a good thing. The detective's conclusions were too heavy for Margarita.

Ricardo, the cabdriver, drove me to the Harlingen airport for my flight to Denver. He didn't talk or sing, and that was unusual. I was adrift in my own jumble of confusion and I didn't push him for conversation. At the airport, we hugged like first cousins.

"If you see Ms. Fuentes, tell her I wish her the best. Whatever happened in Colorado, I know you and her will fix it."

He never actually laid it out for me and the words alone didn't imply anything dramatic. But as I threw my bag in the overhead compartment and sat in the narrow airline seat, I knew I had not been the only passenger Ricardo had driven to the Harlingen airport in the past day or two. And I was convinced Teresa waited in Denver.

The flight home gave me a chance to take stock. The few days with Teresa had healed me, in more ways than one. Yet I convinced myself that I had troubles.

There was a time when the challenges of life appeared as beacons on a hill—bright, shining attractions that drew me to them as surely as insects find a light in the darkness. There is no compact explanation for what happened and I guess it isn't that unusual to ask questions eventually about success and failure, love and hate. We all reconcile the answers with where we are, or we carry on and beg the questions. I flew back from Texas clear in the knowledge that I could not conceive a reconciliation with myself and convinced I had no idea what to do next.

The myths from my youth that I had carried as insurance against self-doubt slipped away with each day that Tino's death remained unsolved.

Memories were freezing into blocks of immobile ice, one indiscernible from another but each a cold gray monolith without feeling or heat.

"Ain't no big thing, *ese.*"

15

---

*I*t was after 9:00 P.M. when the plane touched down at Stapleton. A thunderstorm had exploded over Denver and closed the airport for a few hours. My flight had been delayed in Texas until a traffic controller in the big tower in the sky cleared it for takeoff. The layover didn't help. The plane cruised in sheets of rain as soon as the city lights rose up from the foot of the mountains. We were forced to circle for forty-five minutes. I was hungry, cranky, and stiff from the flight, but I figured I had nothing to lose, and maybe nothing to gain, by checking in with my office.

The uneasy, nervous feeling at the base of my skull told me something was wrong, and I was about fed up with my premonitions of doom. The waiting room had a bad feel to it. I blamed it on the silence, or that a couch's position had been altered, or that the only light shone from under the crack of the door to my office. The cleanup crew usually left the entire building in darkness except for the light over the front door. During the weekend, there was no reason for the light in my office to be on.

I tiptoed to Evangelina's desk and gripped the hammer she kept in a toolbox. I'm not any good at this, I thought. The idea of leaving and calling the cops kicked around in my subconscious for a brief instant. But then, it probably was nothing, and I didn't need any cops busting my balls about a false alarm.

I carried the hammer like a club and eased the door open.

The breeze from an open window whipped around me. Yellow sheets of paper drifted across the room. Each drawer in my file cabinets was pulled open, some dumped on the carpet. Chairs were over-turned, the desk trashed. My law license lay on the carpet surrounded by broken glass. It had been torn from the wall and the frame broken. Someone had spent a good deal of time searching my office and then had left through the window. From the ac-cumulation of mud and water on the carpet, I figured my guest had exited long before the first thunder crash of the rainstorm.

The cops kept me at the office for three hours while they poked around the remains. Although I expected him to plod through the scene in his usual graceful way, Coangelo didn't show up. I insisted I had no idea who might have torn apart the office, and I was of little help to the bored cops who re-sponded to my phone call. We assumed it was just another burglary and I was just another statistic.

I tried to arrange the mess by creating piles of papers that should have made sense. As I picked up muddied copies of letters and rain-stained manila folders, a blurry, obscure picture flirted with my imagination. A tiny voice tried to convince me that an elaborate conspiracy involving Orlie, Hector, and Teresa had been played out in front of my eyes. I kept the vision to myself.

Frank Maldonado, the officer in charge of the crime scene, gave me his card and asked me to call him in a few days after I'd inventoried the place. He wanted a list of missing items and an estimate of my losses. He promised me a copy of his report for my insurance company and we shook hands and parted, each of us satisfied that there wasn't anything else we could do in the little charade of cops and robbers we had been forced into on a late, wet autumn Sunday night.

I harbored a real dislike for the sloppy and amateurish method the burglar had used. It would take days to shape up my office and I wasn't sure I could tell Maldonado what had been stolen. *Oye*, I hardly remembered who my clients were. It seemed impossible to determine whether anything had been taken from their files or the top of my littered desk.

I knew that if my house had been searched, the intruder was more than a simple burglar. I could not have handled the same scene waiting for me when I finally made it home, and I braced for the worst.

The house was secure. During my absence, a chill had settled in the walls. The cold hardwood floor felt like concrete under my shoes. I was uncomfortable and knew I couldn't relax until I had warmth, music, and a drink. When I turned up the thermostat, dusty, stale air flew through the vents and dried my throat. I scribbled a note to myself to call the public-service company for a furnace check.

The taste of Texas had dried on my lips. I dug up a tape of a *conjunto* band from San Antonio. The jubilant music reminded me of sweet Teresa dancing in the shadows of her mother's house.

I started to mix a drink of bourbon and club soda but gave up on the effort when I couldn't find any ice cubes in the freezer. The empty tray lay tossed in the sink. I settled for the last beer.

I sat down at the desk near my bed and leafed through my mail and the newspapers that had piled up on the porch in my absence. I searched for a return to normalcy, the ennui and apathy I had taken for granted only a few weeks before.

A bill from a doctor waited for me. Bernardo's checkup cost me more than three hundred bucks. I couldn't understand it. Doppler Echocardiography—$100.00. Echocardiography, Real-time Image 2D—$175.00. Intermediate SVC, New Patient—$87.50. What was this? The kid sure as hell would make the team, even if I had to be at his practice every night.

Stories about Hector's disappearance were scattered through the pages of the papers. His background had been dissected by various reporters. Their focus usually was a rehash of the judge's consistent commitment to civil rights and equal opportunity, starting with his student-activist days.

Sidebars about Orlie and Tino added morbid spice to the mystery. Orlie was lying low, trying to stay out of the sunshine, where he made a good target. He was impossible to talk to, according to the reporters, but at least he hadn't vanished or been shot. Poor Tino was unearthed and his remains scattered across the headlines for the benefit of the public's right to know. The reporters had a field day with Tino's shady connections, his violent history, and his financial problems. Newspaper and TV hotshots couldn't resist the temptation to jump to conclusions. It was a glorious time for the headline editors. MISSING JUDGE'S CLOSE FRIEND TIED TO WELL-KNOWN GAMBLERS. JUDGE GARCIA VANISHES AFTER THREATS TO FAMILY. RIGHT-WING EXTREMIST GROUPS ON THE RISE IN RURAL AREAS. Each day, another story appeared, without much substance, and my old friend Hector remained a missing person.

The long-awaited baseball team continued as front-page news. There was no decision from the majors about whether Denver would be awarded a team, but that hadn't stopped the fight for the stadium site. The moves and countermoves were into high gear. The various competing groups had all gone public in their attempts to drum up support.

The shining face of Ray Candelaria beamed from the newsprint again, this time arm in arm with Bruce Thompson and Terry Sheehan, fists raised in gestures of strength and confidence. The photo might have been a slightly altered reprint of the one I had seen in Rocky's notebook, yellowed with the passage of time, the men older than the three students celebrating a victory for the people, yet exuberant and cocky in similar ways.

Candelaria aimed his pitch directly at minorities, but his hopes lay with the liberal professional types. He tried to convince people that they could be comfortable about spending several hundred dollars on season tickets because it was a progressive, affirmative action kind of thing to do. The notion had a certain appeal, in a good old-fashioned capitalistic way. What could be more mainstream, more American, damn it, than baseball? It would revitalize the sagging economy! And supporting Candelaria could make a person feel good! I belched beer and tossed the newspapers in the trash.

I rushed into resuscitating the remnants of my career. It was nearly impossible, given the condition of my office. I needed to keep busy, to find distractions from Texas flashbacks and Coangelo's threats. I called clients to let them know I was back and ready for their latest divorce, contract dispute, or codicil for their wills. I made appointments and started sniffing around for new business. I talked to court clerks and convinced a few to put my name back on their court-appointment lists. I showed up at a Hispanic Bar Association meeting and backslapped and glad-handed men and women I hadn't talked to in years.

Evangelina, of course, was a wonder worker. She helped me clean up and I managed to salvage most of my files. As near as we could figure, nothing was missing. She made calls for me, coaxed back less-than-eager clients, and managed to drag up a few referrals from friends she had in other law offices.

She had kept most of my clients on hold during my absence. A "much-needed vacation" was her typical explanation. The few who opted out—Leyba was a good example—had for the most part been thorns in my side and I wasn't really sorry to see them terminated from my accounts, except for the money, obviously.

Mrs. Armstrong's sons bailed her out and helped her find the public defender's office. She had to defend against the various misdemeanors she faced because of the courtroom outburst. She had called and apologized and asked for my help with the charges. Evangelina said I was out of town and that I would talk to her when I returned. Old man Hoskins had thrown her stuff out of the house while she was in jail. She slept on her sister's couch until her application for public housing was approved by the housing authority. Evangelina let me know that Mrs. Armstrong hated the idea of going back to the projects, but there did not seem to be any other choice.

I found a notice from Abrams giving me a day and time to appear for a formal hearing before the Disciplinary Committee. I had two weeks to prepare. The committee accused me of violating the disciplinary rules regarding trial conduct. The language of rule 7-106 intrigued me. "In appearing in his professional capacity before a tribunal, a lawyer shall not engage in undignified or discourteous conduct which is degrading to a tribunal." I didn't think Judge Grant's tribunal could be degraded, but what did I know? That wasn't enough for Abrams. He threw in a charge that was based on a professional canon of ethics that read, "A lawyer should avoid even the appearance of professional impropriety." Now there was a standard of perfection! It seemed to cover about anything I might think of, but I was sure Abrams had more up his sleeve.

Evangelina hadn't been able to convince Abrams to postpone the hearing. The guy apparently held a grudge. Abrams was the prosecutor and three stalwarts of the legal community sat as judge and jury. They would determine my guilt or innocence and make a recommendation to the supreme court, which then had its own shot at me. The court could accept, reject, or modify the recommendation. Abrams's charge included the suggestion that my license should be suspended for at least six months. Six months and I would be through.

He didn't report our little tête-à-tête. That was between him and me and his lawyer.

The guy had a job to do. I tried to tell myself it wasn't personal. The fact that I was a Chicano with no genealogy in the attorney business, no previous history, so to speak, and that Abrams came from a veritable fountain of blue blood should not have anything to do with the disciplinary charges, right? I tried to convince myself that the profession I belonged to included ladies and gentlemen who could put aside the prejudices, narrow-mindedness, and petty conniving of the rest of the world and look at disputes among colleagues with a clear and unjaundiced eye. I tried, I really did. And when that didn't work, I focused on fighting back and looked for a good mouthpiece to win my case.

I dredged up names from my legal aid days. There was a score of damn good attorneys who had worked in the neighborhood offices when the program had a presence in Five Points, the Westside, and a half a dozen other areas that were poor but hip before gentrification threatened their unique existence. A few of them were Establishment types now. That seemed to be the point. I couldn't expect well-educated, bright, hardworking white folks to skate along the lip of penury for the sake of idealism. And I had to be equitable. Many shouldered their fair share of pro bono work, despite the awkward machinations of bureaucratic do-gooders like Tom Robinson. There had to be one that would take on Abrams, regardless of whether he or she appreciated my professional propriety.

Hector's connections might have helped, but I didn't want to call on his friends without his involvement. His disappearance had cramped my preparation. I rejected several options without talking to anybody. There were names I could have used, old favors I could have called in. None seemed right. I wanted to impress the committee, but I wanted to win my case, too.

From my desk in the middle of the construction area that once passed for my office, the hallway stretched in a circle, connecting the space rented by five lawyers, a conference room, and a library. Evangelina sat at her desk, answering the phone and typing pleadings and briefs for the lawyers who office-shared. In addition to me, she worked for two young guys who spent a lot of time on accident cases and workers' compensation claims, one old-timer winding down his practice, and Janice Kendall, my buddy from legal aid.

Her office door was closed. She was quietly preparing for a permanent orders hearing in a typically ugly custody case. She represented the father and had to deal with allegations of drug, child, and wife abuse. She told me once, after she had successfully represented a doctor accused of molesting his infant daughter, that no one really won those kinds of cases. She didn't have to tell me that she would not have been involved unless the old man had something going for him, unless Janice knew for a fact that the best interests of the kids rested with her client—father or mother. Shark seemed like a good bet for me.

I asked her to be my lawyer.

16

A couple of teams played in the World Series, but for the first time in several years I was not interested. There was talk of a dynasty in Oakland, a new murderer's row—false talk, as it turned out. I tried to watch a game. I camped out at one of the dozens of sports bars that had sprung up around town like mushrooms in a pile of manure, and realized I could not focus. The hype and commercials were too much to wade through, and the precise dissection of the game, the analysis by the broadcasters, made me nervous and jumpy. Throw the damn ball and take a cut! I ended up swigging beer and shooting the bull with a raunchy veteran who remembered the good old days when a person had to listen to the Series on the radio. "Seemed more exciting," he mumbled to me after about our sixth long-neck.

This was tough. I hadn't heard a word from Teresa. Orlie's silence bothered me more than his alarmist tirades. And the judge was a seriously missing person. My paranoia wasn't merely creeping around; it was running amok. I caught myself checking out the drivers of cars that stopped next to me at traffic lights. I glanced in store windows at people on the sidewalk, not sure whom I was looking for, not sure what I would do if I saw Teresa's eyes looking at me from among the crowd. "Hello, baby," or "Excuse me, there's a fat detective I need to call"?

I scrounged around for the remnants of family scattered among the debris of what I fondly remembered as my life.

I trooped over to Gloria's house and picked up the boys for the perpetually postponed weekend visit. They were in great shape. Bernardo was busy with football practice. The doctor had decided that no heart murmur existed, after all. At fourteen, my oldest was in better shape than I had ever seen. Eric reluctantly tagged along. An eleven-year-old ought to have better things to do than hang around with the old man.

I handed out the T-shirts I had picked up in Brownsville. One proclaimed the Rio Grande valley THE MOST BEAUTIFUL VALLEY IN THE WORLD and the other trumpeted the tropical delights of South Padre Island. Neither one really grabbed the boys, but they graciously said thanks and asked a few questions about my trip to Texas. I wanted to tell them about beautiful Teresa and her escape into the Texas night, the fight in the bar, and my few hours in the Brownsville jail. But Gloria stood nearby waiting for us to leave, so I skipped out the more interesting details of my alleged holiday.

We visited Jesús. The kids thought Grandpa was good for a few laughs.

"Who are these guys? They look like comic books. Can't you afford to buy them some decent clothes?"

"Dad, those gym shoes cost fifty bucks and Bernie's T-shirt was twenty-five. I paid for both. Eric's stuff, too. Give me a break."

"You guys should check yourselves out. Too much time in the suburbs. Probably listen to New Kids on the Block or some *mierda* like that."

The boys groaned. Eric took up the cause. "Nobody listens to New Kids, Grandpa. Geez, we're older than that."

Jesús laughed. "You guys hungry? Your old man always is; he must have passed that on to you. Had to give you something, I guess."

Yeah, they were hungry.

For about a half hour, we debated where we should eat. I had to consider my father's limited eating capacity and the picky relationship he'd had with food all of his life, plus the boys' refusal to eat anything that wasn't smothered in catsup or spaghetti sauce. We compromised on a cafeteria where everybody could see what they would be eating before I paid for it.

In the line for food, my father spoke to me in Spanish. *"You're in bad trouble, no? This thing with the bar association. Tino. Your disappearing act to Texas. Very serious. You need help?"*

If I asked, the old man would probably pick up a rifle and go with me searching for whoever had decided my life had been too calm for too many years and it was time to stir things around.

We made our way to a table. *"Nothing I can't handle, Jesús."*

156

"Your time in Texas did some good. You almost said that without any gabacho *accent."*

"I had a good teacher."

Bernardo interrupted. "If you keep talking in Spanish, we're going to think you don't want us to hear. What's the deal?"

Jesús put down his fork and stared at his grandson. "The deal is that I think it's time you learned how to speak Spanish. Your father is a disgrace to let you grow up without knowing it."

"I know some words. *¿Cómo estás? ¿Qué paso?* I'm going to take Spanish next semester. If you think I need to learn, maybe you can help me, Grandpa?"

The old man almost blushed. He turned his eyes away.

I said, "That's a great idea, Dad. You can teach these guys how to say the words, so you don't have to worry about any *gabacho* accent."

The old man stuttered, hemmed and hawed—"I ain't no school teacher!"—but the three younger Montez men roped him into helping Bernardo with his homework, mainly with pronunciation, and into giving Eric a few basic phrases so that one day the boy could have a semicoherent conversation in Spanish with his grandfather.

We left his house late that night after watching a couple of rented horror movies that the boys and Jesús insisted on watching.

"Thanks, Dad. See you next week."

"You tell your boys to come over more often. And you call me when you need help. Don't let me learn about it in the newspapers."

* * *

Janice Kendall interviewed me in the quiet of her office. The place implied business and nothing else. When she was working, and that was most of the time, she possessed a seriousness that made me flinch. Her questions were designed to erase the doubts she had about every case. She was the original cynic, a doubting Thomas not convinced by a simple bloody hole in the palm of a hand. If clients lied to her, she disowned them, treated them like dirt, abandoned them to cops and social workers and judges, and turned her back without a second's hesitation. If someone earned her trust, she would hop a plane in the middle of the night to track down a lead, burn candles until dawn at the library reading ancient and complicated opinions of dead judges, and throw glittering pieces of logic at juries until it made absolute sense and the courtroom knew she had created truth. She worked her butt off for her clients.

She ushered me into a leather chair planted directly in front of her desk. I sweated through my shirt and into the chair's armrests. Her quick and staccato interrogation lasted for over an hour, without a break, not so much as a drink of water or a smile. I relived the Armstrong case minute by minute, from the first frantic phone message to the news from Evangelina that my client's sons had bailed her out of jail. Kendall said what I did when Mrs. Armstrong confronted Peters and Hoskins was critical. I explained it, but she didn't like it and I explained it again. She still didn't like it, but we stumbled on.

"What did you say to Peters when you picked up your papers?

"What was he doing while you were talking to him?

"What happened to Hoskins? Why didn't you help him?

"What did you say to Judge Grant?

"What other cases were on the docket?

"Who else was in the courtroom?

"Why couldn't you stop Mrs. Armstrong? Did you even try?

"How could you laugh when the judge demanded order in his court?

"Why, please tell me, did you take a case you hadn't prepared for, you didn't have time for, and a case for which you couldn't come up with a defense?"

I felt like an idiot.

She had me write up a list of people who might vouch for my character. It wasn't long. She said she needed only two or three key witnesses to offset Abrams's certain attempt to assassinate my professional integrity by showing that I was a less-than-desirable element in the general scheme of the legal profession. I gave her the names of judges and lawyers whom I thought might remember me for a few crusading cases I had done in the past or maybe for those that were backbreakingly tough and ended up testing my skills to their limits. She glanced at the list for a second, then hid it in my file with a dozen pages of her notes. Impressed, she was not.

Finally, she called a halt. The interview was over.

I expected her to say thanks but no thanks. She had more important things to deal with, and my story had sounded weak to me. I could imagine what effect it had had on her.

"Louie, it stinks." I slumped into the shiny leather of her chair. "No, no. Not what you did. What the committee is trying to do. And I guess it's Abrams, not the committee. Funny about that guy. I've known him for years. Served on committees and boards with him. Had cases with and against him. He's always treated me like a lady, if you know what I mean. Always a gentleman. Never a word out of line, never anything concrete. But it was there. That brittleness these people have. That invisible line they draw around themselves and that nobody can cross without the right credentials. They squirm when they have to interact with what they think are the lower classes. The guy cannot stand to deal with women or minorities. It bugs the hell out of him. I think you pushed him over the brink." I smiled. "And Peters. What a package! He's a parasite. Had a couple of grievances filed against him, by his own clients. We'll give it a shot, Louie." I shook her hand and left her office in a bit of a daze, thinking I wanted to be a lawyer like her one day.

17

The Monday-night football game held my attention for one quarter until the score climbed out of
hand and the announcers were reduced to incoherent babbling about the weather. The Forty-Niners
tended to do that to announcers, and opponents.

I picked out a record album, blew dust out of its
grooves, turned off the TV noise and cranked up the
stereo's volume. ZZ Top launched into their typical
hard-driving Texas blues–influenced jams that I
could listen to almost any night. Sometimes jazz
didn't cut it. Greasy bikers and skinny women
shared my acquired taste for the bearded rockers. I
considered it my way of crossing one more cultural
barrier. I did what I could in the interest of brother-
hood.

I hadn't bought music in months. I did know that
record albums were already a rarity. Compact discs
or tapes were about all anyone could find in the
music stores. At least that's what Bernie told me.

One of the TV guys appeared to be singing a song.

The phone rang and I wrenched it from its cradle. I toned down the stereo and unconsciously shouted hello into the phone.

Coangelo's rough baritone greeted me with a whisper.

"Montez. I have some bad news, again." Those eyes snapped into my head and I reached for my beer. I forced down a long drink. "We found Judge Garcia. Shot in the head. Maybe you ought to come over here. It's weird."

I felt relief. Nothing about Teresa. Then guilt. I hear about the death of my old *compañero* and all I could think of was the slender *tejanita* who jumped ship in Brownsville and had avoided me since.

"How about Maria? Does she know?"

"I sent a couple of our men over there as soon as I knew who it was. They're watching her. She's been informed. From what I've been told, she's in bad shape. You might need to talk to her."

"What happened?"

"Earlier this evening, a couple of boys were prowling around the gullies by the Jefferson County Airport, off the Boulder turnpike. They saw a car parked along the shoulder of the dirt road that winds around the runways. The judge was in the front seat, his face against the driver's window. He'd been shot in the head. You can imagine how it hit the kids."

It had to have been the maniac who shot Tino. I asked to hear it confirmed by Coangelo.

"How did it happen? The same as Pacheco?"

"This is a little different, Montez. A bullet through the right temple, probably a nine-millimeter. No shotgun. No evidence of a fight. Nothing to indicate that racist vigilantes were involved. In fact, if I was a gambling man, I'd say the judge shot himself."

Maria had been right to cry for her husband the day I tried to talk to her.

"Somebody shot him, like Tino. He wouldn't shoot himself. He wasn't that kind of person. He couldn't . . ."

"That's what I thought, too. At first. We really did want it to be a murder, if you can understand that. He had friends on the force, guys who respected him and the way he treated cops. He tried to deal with the scum they brought in. I can't make it otherwise, though. It looks like a suicide. No note or anything like that. Only the gun in his hand, the angle of the shot, the way his body was found. The judge couldn't handle whatever it was that drove him into hiding a few weeks ago. Of course, that's not official yet, counselor. Your girlfriend hasn't surfaced, so there's still that. Funny how when she's around, your old friends start turning up dead."

I didn't respond. He told me how to find the spot where they had found Hector. I said I would be out there in about a half hour. There was something strange he wanted to show me. He didn't elaborate.

Before he hung up, Coangelo waxed philosophical for a few minutes. The judge's death had affected the cop. His investigation of the body of a man he had worked with and admired opened a nerve he kept hidden under the thick layers of his flesh. That nerve was exposed and raw.

"His funeral will be a big deal. The mayor, city council, all the other judges will be at the service.

Plenty of officers, too. He really had it made, if only he had realized it. There are days, counselor, when I don't much care for my job."

The stretch of dirt road was lighted up like a movie set. I had to identify myself three different times and explain what I was doing out there to three different gruff and serious uniforms from three different jurisdictions before I made it to Coangelo. Hector's gray sports car sat like a black tomb in the center of a ring of police cars, an ambulance, and a tow truck. There was a dark shape curled in the front seat. My breath caught in my throat.

"Don't go over there, Montez. I didn't ask you out here to freak you out about your old friend." He dug around in his overcoat and I thought he was looking for a pack of gum. He pulled out a plastic bag that held a handful of small white objects that were almost iridescent in the moonlight. "What do you think these are?"

I stared at four miniature skulls, each with a silly grin and a slash of color draped over its cranium. They had pins so they could be worn like boutonnieres.

I frowned. Coangelo was not pleased.

"Where did you find these?" I took them from his meaty palm and inspected them up close.

"They were in the judge's inside vest pocket, along with his checkbook. I know Halloween is coming up, but what would he be doing with these things? They for his kids, you think?"

"They could be, Detective. Halloween is close to *Dia de Los Muertos*. These are *calaveras, muertos.*"

164

"Huh?"

"Day of the Dead. A Mexican holiday. A day to remember dead relatives and friends. It's not a big deal in the States. In Mexico, people set up altars with sugar skulls and paper cutouts of skeletons representing those that have passed on. The altars have food for the expected hungry visitors. These kinds of things are little extras. Some enterprising businessman took the idea and made pins to wear around the house on the day the ghosts show up. It's a tradition you probably don't understand."

"I don't give a fuck about any morbid traditions. Every race has its own eccentricities—including Italians."

I shrugged and handed back the tiny skulls.

"I'm investigating a probable suicide. I have to be thorough, you know that."

"I doubt they have anything to do with Hector's death."

"Maybe. I learned a long time ago that the small things are what make the difference—something out of place, something too clean, something tipped over. Skulls in a dead judge's pocket are too eerie for me. But you may be right. They could have nothing to do with this." He tilted his head in the direction of Hector's car.

"Let me see those again. The *calaveras* are usually posed in scenes from everyday life. You know, like a row of skeletons sitting at a bar, drinking, or playing pool, or riding bikes. Don't know if that means the junk we do in life continues after we die, or if it represents the idea that underneath it all we're basically skeletons. Dead. We are all dying, every day."

"You are morbid, Montez." He stared at the tiny masks of death sitting in my hand. "So what do these guys represent? They're only heads, no poses. With hats."

"No, not hats. These are four grinning skulls wearing berets. Red berets."

Maria Garcia had braced herself as best she could, considering what she had been through. Coangelo called ahead and cleared me with his men so I didn't have to wade through any more I.D. checks. But as soon as I walked through the front door and faced Maria, I regretted my decision to try to console her. I had never been close to her, and I wasn't any good at comforting those whose hurt had been bottled up and then released with tears and regrets. I did what I could.

"It can't be true, Luis. Hector wouldn't do that. He loved his daughters too much. He loved me. I know that. He loved us."

"I don't know what happened, Maria. But with Tino dead and Orlie gone and the threats—who knows? It could finally have worn him out. I can't believe it, either. I don't know what to say."

"He would have left word, a note, a letter, something. He wouldn't have run out and, and . . ." She stared without seeing me. "He was a man, Luis. He wouldn't have run away like that, not without telling someone. Not without telling me."

She cried in my arms and I couldn't think of anything that would stop her.

"I'm sorry, Luis. But I have to let this out before I

tell the girls, before I have to explain to them. I have to do my crying now."

"Yes, Maria. Now."

She eventually made a pot of coffee and we sat on the couch drinking cup after cup. I knew I would be up for hours, with a nasty headache from too much caffeine. Drinking the coffee offered a convenient excuse for not talking. Maria insisted on telling me details of the last few days she had spent with Hector.

"The morning after he left, you were here, you remember. I went through everything, trying to figure out what could be going on. I hoped it was a girlfriend or trouble with his cases, anything that I could deal with. I thought if I knew, then we could fix it. Him and me. But there wasn't much."

"Anything that might help with the threats? Orlie's missing. I'm worried about him. Actually, I'm nervous for you and the girls, too. Hell, for me."

"I can't work this out, Luis. I didn't find anything unusual. Except . . . nothing."

I leaned forward and gripped her hands. They were ice-cold.

"What, Maria? What is it?"

"Hector had some bank accounts I didn't know about, a savings and a checking. There's almost four thousand dollars in the savings. The passbook has the girls' names on it. I guess he was planning a big surprise for something in the future." She choked on the words and had to stop. Tears welled up in her eyes again and she shuddered into my arms for a few minutes.

"And the checking account?"

She pointed to a table near the hall doorway. "There were a few registers and some canceled checks. I have no idea what he needed another account for. There weren't many checks written on it. There was only a hundred dollars in it, according to the balance in the book."

I leafed through a pile of envelopes and sheets of paper. Bank statements and canceled checks were stuffed into a manila envelope. Maria was right. The account had not been very active. Hector had made a few deposits each month and then apparently wrote one check each month. What Maria had failed to tell me was that the monthly deposits added up to a thousand dollars a month. And each month, around the fifteenth, Hector wrote a check for one thousand dollars to the bank that managed the account. Scribbled on some of the checks were the words *money order*.

I shuffled more papers, looking for a receipt, a note, anything that could help me understand why Hector had bought a thousand-dollar money order each month. I was about to give up when a yellow slip of paper floated out of a bundle secured with a rubber band. I picked it up off Maria's spotless carpet. It was the second page of a money order, the page that served as a copy for the buyer, with impressions from the first page transferred by a piece of carbon paper. It was difficult to read, but I could see that the money order had been made out to the order of Corsican Plaza Enterprises.

I didn't need to find any more receipts or checks. Each month, Hector had paid someone connected to the building ownership almost twice the usual rent of one of the Corsican Plaza apartments. I let my imagination go. I asked myself how long Hector had been renting peace of mind from his old buddy Tino the apartment manager. One thousand a month for twenty years could back up a lot of greyhound bets. One thousand a month for twenty years could help pay for the expensive habits of young secretaries titillated by the macho bluster of the old-time Chicano radical. One thousand a month for twenty years.

I didn't leave Maria until after midnight. She calmed down and we constructed a plan for talking to the girls and making arrangements for the funeral. She asked me to deal with the bar association and Hector's staff. Of course, I agreed. We concentrated on numbing details.

A pair of policemen were permanently stationed in her front yard and I was sure that nothing would happen to her. The white-hooded vigilantes had turned into a wild dream from many years ago and now I had to confront a nightmare whose meaning held implications far greater than I could ever have imagined. I had to find Orlie.

I talked myself into stopping for a drink. It didn't take much effort. The coffee had me jumpy and strung out. Hector's death and Maria's suffering must have had something to do with it, too. The last time I had a beer in the Dark Knight, Tino and Teresa found me and we partied through the night. It seemed right to visit the same bar on the night another friend's body had been found.

There were a few holdovers from the game, but the place was relatively quiet. The joint offered dollar shots of schnapps after each touchdown and a well-stocked buffet table of chicken wings and nachos. The place filled up during the game, but, as soon as the final whistle blew, the fans usually cleared out. It was Monday, after all.

I found a table near the back. I chugged one beer and had a good start on my second when I thought I should try to figure out a few things. I wrote a few disjointed paragraphs in a small memo book I carried in my pocket. Hector's checking account. The money order. Orlie and the threats. Rocky's journal. That's all I could do. Words, a string of non sequiturs. I couldn't make any connection.

A trio of men crashed through the front door. They were laughing, shoving and punching each other. Drunk and boisterous, they demanded beers from the bartender and change for the jukebox. Their colorful T-shirts and expensive athletic shoes looked out of place in the smoky bar. I recognized Humberto Gonzales more from the pushy way he commanded his buddies than from any physical trait. I rubbed my ribs and finished off my beer.

I had a strange high. Maria's coffee and the beer buzzed around my ears. The scene of Hector's body and the dozen cops looking for clues played over in my head every five minutes or so, and Maria's pain engulfed me in the same terror and loneliness she already knew. I had to do something, and right then the best thing I could see myself doing involved choking the life out of the two-bit hoodlum who had strategically placed one of his high-priced shoes in the middle of my rib cage.

I ordered another beer and watched the men. They were intent on drinking and didn't pay any attention to the few of us in the bar. They hassled the bartender, but he could handle it. Another half hour and it would be time to close. One of the men weaved from the bar to the rest room. A few minutes later, he made his way back to his stool and Hummy decided to follow his lead.

"Order me one more, guy. Need to see a man about an elephant." Hummy's buddies ignored him.

He banged into the rest room's door and tripped inside. I was directly behind him. He started to fall and I grabbed him under the arms.

"Whoa, buddy. Take it easy." I held on to his arms.

"Yeah. Thanks, man. I'm okay." He tried to jump free, but I stuck with him. Whatever kind of coffee Maria used, I made a note to buy a year's supply. I felt as if I could hold on to a freight train. The perplexed Hummy waved his arms, but my fingers dug into his biceps. I twisted him around to face me.

"Hey, man. What gives? I said I'm okay."

It was not the time to talk. I yanked him into me and slammed my knee in his groin. He fell forward, clutching his midsection, the blood draining from his face. A gurgle escaped his lips, but he couldn't make any other sounds.

"You probably don't know me, Hummy. But a while back, you were doing a job on a friend of mine, and you managed to fuck me up, too. Now we're even, asshole."

He strained to speak and a whisper squeaked out from clenched lips. "What . . . what do you want?"

"Talk to me, Hummy. What's the deal with you and Orlie Martinez? Why were you shoving him around?"

It took him several minutes to blubber more than a few words at a time, and I was worried that his friends might finally notice his absence and wander into the toilet looking for him. Hummy wasn't saying much and it looked as if his strength might return any second.

I couldn't help it. I stood over him and remembered the nights of sweating out the pain in my upper torso, the burning I felt when I took a deep breath, and the tablets of oxycodone. I kicked him in the ribs and a dull thud echoed from the tile walls. Hummy's eyes glared like a highway flare for an instant, then he passed out. "We're not even anymore, asshole. I guess you owe me one."

18

———————————◆———————————

My hearing was held in a downtown building not far from Teresa's office at Graves, Snider. The suite housed investigators, staff attorneys, prosecutors, and support. A conference room with a library served as the venue for the hearing. In the interest of cleanliness, the supreme court set up the Disciplinary Committee in its own environment and let it do pretty much as it pleased until it forwarded recommendations on each of its cases.

Janice and I arrived a little early. She had kept me informed about what she intended to do, but a nagging doubt stuck with me, the way most clients must feel before they start a legal proceeding that might change their lives. I was antsy, uptight. She maintained her sense of purpose. She prepared exhibits, arranged her notes, reviewed witnesses' statements.

Abrams failed to acknowledge my existence, but he was very cordial with my attorney, almost talkative. The three members of the panel showed up and, almost before I realized it, the hearing started.

My judges were three lawyers unhindered by past professional indiscretions and bolstered by well-established reputations for competency. Karen Beatty served as presiding officer. She gave an introduction to each witness and made decisions if there were evidentiary disputes among the lawyers. These hearings were informal, although every one who testified had to be sworn to tell the truth. Two Anglo males completed the panel. I actually trusted their collective judgment. Only Abrams cast a shadow over the hearing.

Abrams presented his case in an hour. He had Gaston Peters testify. It was a simple story and Peters recounted it in a straightforward, monotonous tone. He pronounced most of his vowels in a funny way, using a lot of his nasal passages as if he came from Boston or some other strange place. I knew he had been born and raised in scrubby eastern Colorado, out where the only Mexicans were farmhands without immigration papers and the Indians who had once called the high plains home were now remembered only because a small museum displayed a dusty collection of arrowheads.

First, I had presented a frivolous defense. "This was a simple eviction, and Mr. Montez dragged it out for what seemed like hours. His client had no lease, no right to be in the premises if the landlord wanted her out. That's the way it is in Colorado. Mr. Montez has done housing cases in the past; he knows landlord-tenant law. He wasted our time."

Second, I encouraged my client to disrupt the proceedings. "The judge was giving his decision from the bench. Mr. Montez was talking excitedly to his client, almost to the point that we couldn't hear what the judge was saying. Then she stood up and started hollering at the judge, and at my client and me. He didn't do anything to stop her. In my opinion, he egged her on. I had the distinct impression that she was looking to him for direction. In fact, before she attacked my client and me, Mr. Montez said something to her and then turned her in our direction."

Third, I added insult to injury by gloating over Hoskins and Peters after they had been knocked down by Mrs. Armstrong. "I thought he would help us. But he actually laughed in our faces. Mr. Hoskins was in serious condition. We still don't know the extent of his injuries. But Montez laughed. I was shocked. Then he threatened us. He said if we didn't let his client stay in the house, he would tell some wild story to the press and turn his client loose on us again. I had never seen such unprofessional conduct in all the fifteen years I've been a lawyer. It was a sad day for the legal profession."

I almost puked.

The three panel lawyers looked at me in unison and I thought I saw them shake their heads in pity and sorrow. Then Shark grabbed hold of Peters.

"Isn't it true that Mr. Montez tried to restrain Mrs. Armstrong? That, in fact, he held her and tried to pacify her, without any help from the court or you?"

Peters mumbled. "I didn't see anything like that."

"And isn't it also true that Mrs. Armstrong hit Mr. Montez?"

"I saw him fall on the floor. I don't know why he did that."

Janice and I sat in chairs around the large oblong table that served as the boundary between the witnesses and parties and the panel. She wanted to stand up and approach the witness; she wanted to stare in his face and make him sweat. However, the way the hearing was set up, she had to remain seated and direct her questions at Peters from across the table. She hunched forward, pointed her pen at Peters, and did the best she could under the circumstances to let him know that she would not let him off easily.

"Mr. Peters. You said my client wasted time in the courtroom. Don't you mean that he wasted time because the defendant decided to exercise her right to a trial? You do agree that she has a right to a trial, to ask a judge to make a decision about her case?"

Peters paused for a few seconds, then launched into his tirade. "We wasted time because Montez didn't have a case. He should have known that. Neither my client, the court, nor I should have to put up with listening to somebody's ranting and raving only because she doesn't want to be evicted. If I had my way, we wouldn't have trials in these kinds of cases. They waste everybody's time and money, including the court's."

Janice shuffled through her papers and I could feel my heart racing. The night before, when I had had trouble falling asleep, I'd told myself to cool it. I had stumbled into being a lawyer; I could stumble into something else. Maybe it was time. I didn't really need the grief. I could teach, open up a liquor store, write a book. Hell, if Abrams won, he wanted six months only, not my life, although there wouldn't be anything to come back to after six months. I caught myself holding my breath. I let it out too quickly, in a loud gush of air. Janice gave me this look, like what the hell was I doing, and then she went back to work.

"Your complaint against Mrs. Armstrong wasn't based on nonpayment of rent, was it?"

"No."

"And you didn't allege that she had violated a term of any tenancy agreement?"

"There wasn't any agreement. There wasn't any lease. That was the point."

"Exactly. You filed the case simply because you wanted her out. You didn't allege any reason."

"In this state, landlords don't need a reason."

"It had nothing to do with her race?"

"Please, Ms. Kendall. That's ridiculous. Mr. Hoskins has tenants all over town, of every race and color." He smiled. He thought that was Janice's shot and it made him relax.

"Well then, why, Mr. Peters? Why was it so important that Mrs. Armstrong leave the house she had lived in for years?" A basic principle of the art of cross-examination is that you don't ask "why" questions. I wiggled my butt in the chair, hoping I could relieve my anxiety.

"It was a business decision. That's all. Mr. Hoskins was selling the property. The buyer insisted that the house be vacant before the deal could be finalized. I suppose the buyer thought it would be easier that way, cleaner."

"No ongoing tenant to deal with, so the house could be demolished and whatever development was planned could begin. Is that right?"

"Something like that."

Her eyes brightened. She loved this.

"Are you familiar with a company called New Properties, Ltd.?"

Peters took his time about answering. "What's that have to do with this?"

"Please answer the question, Mr. Peters."

"I don't see what relevance . . ."

"This is an informal hearing. You know I have quite a bit of latitude here. New Properties, Ltd. What is that?"

He looked at the panel for help. Maybe they had a rope to reel him away from the Shark.

Karen Beatty cleared her throat. "You can proceed, but keep your questions within reason, Ms. Kendall. We have to carry on."

"Certainly. New Properties, Ltd., Mr. Peters."

"If you're asking me for a list of my clients, I don't have to give you that."

"How about something that's public record?" She held a bundle of official-looking documents. "Aren't you one of the incorporators of New Properties, Ltd.? At least that's what's listed on the articles of incorporation that were filed in the secretary of state's office."

"Yes, that's right. I'm involved in quite a few enterprises. I am a lawyer, after all." He twisted his neck in an obvious show of disapproval.

"Yes, Mr. Peters, so I've been told. This particular enterprise is very interesting, however. Tell me, did Mr. Hoskins know that while you were representing him, while you were trying to evict his tenant, it was your company he was negotiating with for the purchase of the land?"

"I did not negotiate with Hoskins. New Properties has its own lawyer for that. I'm on the board of directors, that's all."

"That's all, Mr. Peters?" She did not look at him. She stared directly at Beatty. "Tell us, please. Did your client Hoskins know that as a member of the board of directors of New Properties you insisted that the house had to be vacant before there could be a deal?" Beatty frowned, the creases in her forehead wrinkling her skin like an accordion. My lawyer pressed forward. "Don't you think that's very convenient? Maybe too convenient? Not only does your own company bargain with one of your clients, you stir up a little extra business by offering to handle the eviction that you said was necessary in the first place."

Peters was sweating now. If Janice could have stood up, she would have been about six inches from his face. Abrams made a gesture as if he was going to say something, maybe offer a word of guidance for Peters. Beatty shook her head to let him know that his interruption would not be appreciated.

Janice continued. "Tell me, Mr. Peters, do the words *conflict of interest* have any meaning for you?"

Of course, the fact that Peters was less than innocent did not necessarily mean that I was off the hook. It's not inconceivable that two lawyers could

179

be unethical in the same case at the same time. Janice's digging into Peters's business dealings had paid off, however. The wind had been let out of his sails and he was sinking fast by the time the panel excused him with a warning that he would now be the subject of his own investigation. Abrams babbled about irrelevancy and immateriality, but he had lost his audience. The rest of the day was Shark's show.

She presented one of the bailiffs, who testified that I had been a great help with my client. Judge Grant's clerk testified, quite vocally, I thought, that I was always a gentleman in the courtroom, that I treated the judge and her with the greatest respect, and that she had not seen anything unprofessional about what I had done on the day of the trial. Janice had tried to bring in Judge Grant, but he managed to be on vacation and out of the city. She made a point of reminding the panel that Grant had not filed a complaint.

Then a parade of character witnesses marched through the hearing. People I had known over the years—from legal aid, the lawyers who shared offices with Janice and me, and a pair of attorneys I had argued against in the courtroom. Old Judge Garrison from the court of appeals came through and testified about my work on one of his committees that cooked up schemes on how to make the court system more accessible to the public, particularly for litigants who didn't speak English. I had forgotten about that.

The last witness was a surprise to me. The old man shuffled into the hearing room and sheepishly looked at me. I squinted at Janice. She whispered in my ear. "He insisted he wanted to help. It's okay. He'll do fine." Jesús Genaro Montez swore to tell the truth and then I had to help him to the chair where he would testify. The first words out of his mouth clinched it for me. "Louie is a little crazy, but he would never do anything stupid. Crazy, yes. Stupid, no." Thanks, Dad.

19

I wouldn't learn the panel's decision for several weeks. Meanwhile, I was allowed to continue with the never-ending process of managing my business.

Evangelina arranged appointments and dropped files on my desk that I had to review. I worked late, catching up and starting on new cases. A few of the clients who had bailed out while I had been otherwise occupied renewed our relationship. It felt good to stay busy drafting pleadings, researching an arcane contract provision, and trying to meet deadlines imposed by courts or clients.

The call from Gregorio Leyba was the most surprising. The old man had dumped me, although I had followed through on his bankruptcy. His backside had been saved by my paperwork, yet as soon as I was in too deep to make a fight out of it with him, he wanted his retainer back, claiming I had delayed too long. I gave him back half of the two grand and considered myself better off to be rid of him. Now he was back.

"*¡Compadre!* How are you? I need your help, Louie." As simple as that, as if he had not fired me, as if he had not threatened Evangelina when she'd refunded only half of his money.

"What do you want, Gregorio? I'm busy."

"Hey, Louie. Don't be a goof. You need work. You're one step ahead of your own bankruptcy. But that shouldn't matter, man. We've known each other for years. Just because the last thing didn't work out, no hard feelings, eh? Business is like that. We're businessmen."

It had to be the mercenary streak that was branded into me in law school. There was no other explanation. I let him talk me into doing more work for him. I thought to myself all during his blathering that I really didn't like the man. But he was right. This was business. I didn't have to like my clients—hell, I didn't even have to believe them. I merely had to work for them.

Leyba had a bad case of the baseball crazies, as did half the rest of the city. He wanted a concession operation at the new stadium. I pointed out to him that Denver had not yet been awarded a team. That announcement was months away. There wasn't a final choice on the stadium site, and it would be years before anyone had a chance to bid on concessions. None of that fazed him.

"I'm ready to start the groundwork now, Louie. I need contracts, advice about the bidding process. You know some of the people that I will have to deal with later, like Candelaria and his crew of hustlers. I have to hustle them. It's a great opportunity, but I need to swing into gear. What do you say?"

Ah, baseball. The two-out rally. The called third strike. The diving slide into second that stretches a single into a double. The beer. Shorts and halter tops. The millions spent on player salaries. The millions more made by owners. I love the game.

I allowed myself to fall into the idea of having something to do with the new team, not because I was a hotshot speculator or knew the right connections or simply because I expected to make a bundle. It came down to the fact that maybe I could snatch a couple of season tickets out of whatever it was Leyba thought he was going to do. The last remnant of my soul was on the trading block. The devil could have it for box seats along the third-base line.

"What's the deal, Gregorio?"

And the perennial Northside con man filled me in on his plan to sell burritos and tamales at the games, to try to compete with the hot dogs, pizza, and peanuts that were certain to be offered.

"Not simple burritos, Louie. Baseball burritos. Small ones to be eaten like chicken nuggets, you know what I mean? Special salsa, maybe a hot dog burrito. For tradition. And tamales, tacos. Foods that go good with beer. But with the fan in mind. And I've already been making connections. I need a shove in the right direction, that's all."

It was an interesting story, involving characters I knew, some in roles I hadn't suspected. He had started weeks ago, meeting with various groups of people who had an interest in the new team, including Candelaria and a few of his backers, when he realized he needed to know more about the legal potholes. That's where I came in. I made an appointment to see him later in the month. Before I hung up, I let him know the rules.

"No hassles this time. No refunds on retainers or anything else. And Gregorio, if you run down here demanding to see me, I'll personally throw your ass out. ¿Entiendes?"

"Compadre. I'm hurt. But you're the lawyer, man. Your rules. No problem."

Coangelo and his buddies were looking for two people—Orlie Martinez and Teresa Fuentes. He stopped by one Indian summer afternoon when the moon was high above the snowy mountain peaks along the horizon. He sweated in his heavy overcoat, his breath tortured. The man was a heart attack waiting to happen. One more cinnamon roll or a mad rush up a flight of stairs in pursuit of a perpetrator and that would be it. The detective was convinced that Teresa and Orlie each had had a part in Tino's death and that Judge Garcia was also involved. He figured Hector couldn't take it anymore, so the judge finished himself off before it turned really ugly and dragged him down. I argued, insisted on my friends' innocence. Neither one of us was convinced.

"I think Fuentes learned that Orlie, Tino, and the judge were responsible for Ruiz's death. I figured that much from Ruiz's notebook."

He earned some of my respect for that. Either he had reached Margarita and she'd let him see what Rocky had written or he sneaked into her house and read what he wanted while she was teaching fourth graders. Either way, he had shown initiative.

"Those guys were going to do something at the conference, something that Ruiz had a problem with. It went bad, somebody made a mistake, and Ruiz ends up shot. Maybe there were vigilantes. It could have been that the Chicanos cornered them, and one of those punks in hoods was supposed to be hit. Only poor Ruiz was in the way and he's the one that dies a martyr for the cause."

He chewed gum with slow, lazy movements of his jaws while he talked. He drove me crazy but I tried to remember that I was cool, man. Somewhere in my past I had been a *vato*, a wise guy, a kid regularly hassled by cops for walking the streets, and so I never lost my perspective. Maintain, man, that was the key.

"Your girlfriend figures this out. She's very bright, so I've been told. Knew the judge in law school, probably learned from him that the old gang was around. Funny how you guys never strayed far from one another. Kept close all these years. Ms. Fuentes lands a job in Denver. Really went all out to make sure she found work in this area."

"It's not that surprising, Coangelo. She was at the top of her class. Any firm in the country would have wanted her."

"Yeah. And she chose Denver. Like I say, counselor, it's the little things that I pay attention to. Maybe I'm missing the most obvious, but I don't think so. She could have done nicely in Dallas or Houston or Austin or San Antonio. She ends up in Denver, along with four of her dead father's best friends."

He didn't say it, but in my head I added it for him.

She had failed to tell any of us that she was Rocky's daughter.

"Then the threats start. Drives Martinez nuts. Then the judge, and Tino probably. They get threats, too. Everyone except you, Montez. She likes you, though. She pals around with Pacheco for a while, then you two become an item. Show up at her law firm's parties, hang around town at a few of your favorite bars."

"I know all this, Detective."

"How much do you know, Montez? Maybe she let you in on more than you've told me so far. Why don't you let it out, and we can end this right here."

"This is your show. You're big on theories. I'd like to hear yours."

"Okay, counselor. It's like this. Your girlfriend and the judge had a scam going on with Martinez and Pacheco. She learned something from the judge in law school—something about her father's death. It fell apart, turned crazy. Tino ends up dead. That was more than Garcia bargained for. Now, either Orlie's hiding out, afraid to come to us, or he's already dead and his body will turn up one of these days, too."

"You can't really believe that Teresa shot Tino. It's crazy."

"We live in a crazy world, counselor. But let me make it very clear for you. Your girlfriend is wanted. She's the number-one suspect. I will find her. She's in town—looking for Martinez, no doubt. If she contacts you, you better let me know, counselor. Don't do anything else to jeopardize your law license. Murder isn't in the same class as disrupting a small-time county court hearing. Don't fuck up, Montez."

20

◆

Evangelina told me she appreciated the fact that I had thrown myself into the resurrection of my practice. It meant steady work for her. I gave her the benefit of the doubt and convinced myself that she cared about me. I tried to sound sincere when I said I was turning over a new leaf.

The truth was that I couldn't think of a better way for Teresa to make contact. She wouldn't track me down in a bar—too public. She might try catching me at my house, and I waited nervously a few nights for her knock. I faced up to the fact that I felt more at home in my office. I decided I would work late for as many nights as it took until she found me. There was no doubt in my mind that she would look for me.

It was also the best way to wait for Orlie.

I peered through the blinds and saw only the silhouettes of bushes and trees—shadows in the dark.

Hours earlier, I had wrapped myself into a client's claim that the contract she negotiated for printing services for her restaurant had to be re-written. Too many loopholes and unanswered questions. Apparently, the printer wanted a new deal, too. My job was to manipulate a happy ending for a relationship that had barely started but already was in disarray. I drafted different contract clauses to give the client a few options. I was in the middle of a fourth version of the agreement when the ringing phone brought me back to the bright glare of my office in the otherwise-dark building.

Her voice wound around my insides like the cord dangling from the phone. An incoherent mix of pictures rushed through my head: her face on the pillow next to me in the amber light of a Texas morning; her laughter as I tried to learn how to ride a horse. These were easy to handle. But Coangelo's words—"number-one suspect . . . murder"—reverberated like thunder across the mountains and drowned out all the other memories.

"Luis. You're there. Good. I'll come by in a few minutes. Is anyone around?"

"I'm alone, Teresa."

I shut the blinds. The wind had picked up and the short spell of warm weather had blown over the mountains. Storm clouds covered the sky. Odds were good that by morning snow would dust the streets in a white cover of moisture and quiet.

It was useless to continue with my work. I had to be ready to talk with her. I went over the notes I had written, but they only reminded me that I couldn't figure this out.

I unlocked the main entrance and waited for her

at the front of my desk. Standing there, waiting, I did not know whether or how seconds passed or hours. She walked straight in to my office, stopped when she was inches from me, and smiled. I thought I heard the Al-Re-Ho radio again. The light from her eyes triggered the old visions. The unrelenting passion that lay barely beneath the surface of her skin filled the room. She overwhelmed me. I fought against slipping back into the dream we had created on her grandfather's ranch.

The long black coat was too light for the weather. She had bunched her hair on the top of her head so that it was out of her way. It looked great. I could see more of her cheekbones and her smooth, soft temples. She started to shed the coat, then changed her mind and kept it on. She hugged me. I held her, put my arms inside her coat, and rubbed against her sweater, cashmere and black.

"Luis. We have so much to talk about."

"Yes. We didn't do much of that in Texas."

"We didn't cover everything. Do you have a smoke?" That was a surprise. I realized how little I knew about her.

"No. There might be some around. We can look."

"That's all right. I'm nervous, that's all. It feels like years since Texas."

"Yes. Years. What happened after you ditched Coangelo? I thought you were ready to come back with him. I thought you wanted to clear this up."

"Why waste time, right, Luis? We might as well get to it. But the truth is, I don't know. I don't have a precise explanation. The men at the bar were friends of my father, and my grandfather. They helped me out of there. They hid me for a few days, then I left Brownsville. I didn't want any trouble for them. It happened so fast in the bar, there wasn't anything I could do except go along with them. I thought I could return to Denver and straighten it out. I plan to talk to that detective, but I need to learn a few more things."

"Teresa, you can't hide from the police for much longer. They concluded that you killed Tino, that you and the judge and Orlie are part of a conspiracy of some sort."

"You don't believe that. Luis?"

The icy sleet that had started to splatter against the window was clean and pure compared to my thinking. I couldn't answer her. I didn't know what to believe. I wanted to stare at her eyes and not say a word and hope she would show me the truth. She put her hands in her coat pockets. I saw a bulge in one and knew it was a gun. She could shoot me as part of some convoluted revenge for Rocky and I couldn't stop her.

I turned my back to her and walked to my chair. I was about to tell her that I might have a pack of cigarettes stashed in the bottom drawer.

I flew forward, bouncing off my desk. It happened so quickly that I did not have time to stop myself. My head smashed against the wall. In my stunned and dizzy condition, I saw a smear of blood on the wall from my head.

"Teresa . . . what . . ."

A shout echoed through the office. Grunts and the quick rush of expelled breath let me know that a fight was happening behind me. I tasted blood at the corner of my mouth. My left eyebrow felt as if it had been chopped off with a knife. I leaned against the wall for an instant, expecting the explosion of a gun and a flash of pain to tear into my body.

"Okay, Louie. Take it easy. Turn around, real slow." Orlie's voice was shaky and tight as if he had been living on bad dope and no sleep. He held a gun against Teresa's pretty temple.

"Don't do anything crazy, Orlie."

"This is way past crazy, Louie. Your girlfriend here fixed everything." He shook his gun in her face. "She managed to fuck it all with her spooky phone threats. She flushed out Tino and Hector. Yeah, she fixed everything good."

I shuffled toward him, an inch at a time. I wasn't sure what I could do, but I had to move the gun away from Teresa's face.

I stalled for time until I could think of something. "How did it get this far, Orlie? Rocky and you and I were brothers, man. We grew up together. What happened to you?"

"What a *tonto* you are sometimes, Louie. Brothers! That's good, man. Everyone's a bro, a *carnal*. You and Hector and that jerk Tino. You all had it made. And Orlie Martinez, what does he have? In case you hadn't noticed, Louie, I don't have a goddamned thing."

He grabbed Teresa by the shoulders as if he might kiss her. Then he started to shake her. Her hair fell out of its bun and across her shoulders. Her head rolled from side to side. Whimpers escaped from her tight jaws.

192

"Orlie!" My shout made him stop. I kept on talking. "When Leyba said that you were at the meeting with him and Candelaria, it almost made sense. You didn't have any money. You've never had money. And yet you wanted in on the stadium deal. Orlie Martinez, urban crusader and would-be investor."

His only response was a glassy stare. He smiled at Teresa. I talked some more.

"Your partner Hummy Gonzales can be very descriptive about your relationship with him. It's all the cops will need to bring you in, Orlie. He won't take the rap for you."

"That fucking Hummy. He had to act tough, and you had to jump in like a comic-book hero. I knew it was you who nailed him in the bar. He must have spilled his guts."

"Enough to figure out that you and he had a business arrangement and you were holding out on him. I ended up with cracked ribs because of your drug deals. You were selling to the kids in your center, Orlie, to the kids you said you were trying to help. No matter how tough it got for you, how could you do that?"

His eyes were red and wild. He shoved Teresa into a chair and motioned me closer to her.

"What the fuck do you know? I've worked for those people all my life, and what does it mean? Nothing. Not a damn thing. They're punks. Niggers and junkies and whores. They're going to buy dope whenever they want. They don't care how they get it. It was time I made a little money."

"You used to talk about revolution. About justice

193

for the people. You were one of the Berets. It didn't mean anything. It always was a scam for you, wasn't it?"

Teresa's voice sounded tiny and weak. "It was more than that, Luis. Rocky knew Orlie wasn't what he pretended to be. It was there in his notebook, but it didn't make sense. I couldn't sort it all out at first. There were too many pages missing. Orlie was an informant for the police. He made a little extra money back then. Rocky busted him. This savior of the people killed my father to protect his ass. He couldn't risk exposure. He had too much invested."

Orlie's face didn't change. He looked exhausted, worn out by the weight of the secrets he had carried for years and the double life he had created for himself. Now he was acting out the last scenes of his creation and it didn't matter how it ended.

"A couple of real smart Chicanos. Just like good old Rocky. He was going to lay it out for Hector and Tino. He thought he could talk us out of torching the administration building. He really believed they would stop me. That was his problem, his weakness. He counted too much on other people. He always was a weakling. But I was a step ahead of him. I had Hector and Tino convinced that Rocky was the agent." He slapped himself on his chest. "I was the *jefe*. They believed anything I told them. They didn't expect it to go as far as it did that night we put him on trial. He tried to fight back. I was kicking his ass and he's talking about the people, *¡la raza!* What a sap!" Teresa flinched at his words. I wanted him to shut up, but I knew if he did he would kill us.

"I tried to scare him off, force him to leave. I started

shooting, to wake him up, to show him I could do it. We were serious, and the fool wanted to talk about commitment and the movement and all that other gibberish. Hector freaked, of course. He sat in the car while Tino and I had our fun. And then that stupid son of a bitch Pacheco blew it and Rocky went down, like that!" He snapped his fingers. "Tino had the bad habit of going to extremes. That stopped the Guerilleros, the fire, everything."

Teresa's eyes swelled with tears. She finally knew the truth about her father.

Orlie grinned at Teresa. "I'm surprised Tino didn't tell you all about it. He loved to talk. That's why Hector and I paid him—to keep his mouth shut. I should have finished him off years ago. His ambition eventually threatened the land deal. My one chance over the hump, to quit the day-to-day trash I've had crammed down my throat. Tino thought he could cash in on what I had going for myself. What a sorry ass. He bowed out at the right time. I guess I owe you something."

He wasn't making sense, but I didn't have time to clear it up. I stood next to Teresa. Orlie weaved directly in front of both of us. I thought I might jump at him, try to slap the gun out of his hand. I was diagramming moves in my head when Teresa's foot shot out from under her chair and caught Orlie on the ankle. She knocked his legs out from under him and he fell in a heap. He awkwardly raised himself back to his feet. His gun waved in the air. I finally stirred and grabbed his arms. He turned and swung his hand. The butt of the gun smashed into the cut over my eye and I felt a new surge of blood gush out.

Nausea swept over me and I was disoriented and useless. Orlie shouted, kicked, and stomped like a madman.

The gunshot whistled in my ears and echoed in my brain. The madman stiffened, then collapsed. I slid off his back, darkness creeping into the outer rims of my eyes. I stared up at beautiful Teresa holding a gun in her hand aimed directly at my heart.

O rlie Martinez died before the ambulance made it to Denver General. I was luckier. I needed only a few stitches over my eye.

And it took only a lake of whiskey to burn Teresa out of my system. The last I heard, she had taken a job with a civil-liberties outfit in the Rio Grande valley, representing refugees and immigrants, demanding asylum and decent housing. Rocky's penchant for clichés such as *justice* and *equality* seemed to have rubbed off on her.

Orlie had taken the myth of the movement from me. The illusions I had had about those years died next to him on my bloodstained office carpet. Los Guerilleros, Orlie, Tino, and Hector, the marches and picket lines—they lost their hold over me when the ugly truth about Rocky's death crawled out of Orlie's mouth. The one thing I had found was Rocky. I had forgotten what he had meant to me, what it was that made his life important. Now it was solid in my heart and Orlie could not take that. Rocky was the real movement and I guess I finally figured out what it was all about.

A few days after the midnight clash in my office, I drove Teresa to the airport for her trip home. We couldn't think of many things to say to each other and it dawned on me that we never really had had much to say. I was seconds from telling her how much I needed her and how we could have a good thing if we gave it a chance, but the words never came out. You see, all the time that I was staring into her eyes, I wanted to ask about the telephone threats, how she'd disguised her voice and how she'd come up with the scheme to flush out her father's killers from twenty years of hiding. I wanted to know whether it was she or Orlie who searched my office. I watched her face for an answer to Hector's suicide, and a reason for Orlie thinking that he owed something to Teresa. And I needed to know that it was Orlie who had shot Tino. I needed to know and I never asked.

"Thank you, Luis. Look us up when you're down in the valley. Margarita tells me she missed you after you left."

"And you, Teresa? How do you feel?" I placed my finger on her cheek and felt the warmth and the softness. I ached for that sensation, missed it already, and she hadn't boarded her plane.

She didn't directly answer my question. "I hope you understand why I can't stay."

No, I didn't understand, but I also didn't demand an explanation. I think Texas women scared the hell out of me.

* * *

"If you don't mind me saying, you ought to go on a diet, Detective. You don't look healthy."

Coangelo had picked up the habit of stopping by for a few minutes. Not often. I could count on seeing him every ten days or so. We talked about politics and baseball and once or twice we grabbed a bite of lunch, although with him a bite could mean half a side of beef.

"It doesn't matter. I'm retiring in a few months. Figure I'll eat myself into oblivion somewhere along the coast of Baja California. I can't wait to leave this city . . . all the scumbags, hoodlums, and freaks. It does something to a person's heart."

"Save it. I've heard it. You won't be gone for long. Look me up when you're back. We can take in a Zephyrs game."

"If I return, that's a deal, counselor. That is, if you can find time to fit me in between all the immigration hearings you're doing these days. Where did that come from?"

I shrugged. "A new line of business. It's a few extra bucks. The undocumented are entitled to a mouthpiece. Hey, we all have to make a living."

He chugged out of my office. Apparently, I had a new friend, an Italian cop who weighed too much and thought I hung out with lowlifes. He also didn't approve of my taste in women.

Coangelo's report on the case concluded that Orlie had planned to burn down one of the university buildings to set up busts on the student leaders at the conference. His warped perspective must have made him think he could have basked in the glory of bringing down the revolution. It was to be his break into the big time and out of the movement. Rocky tried to stop it. I guess he did.

Evangelina buzzed on the intercom. "Excuse me, Louie. You have two calls out here. One is from Mrs. Armstrong. Something about a guy who sold her a washer and dryer and now a 'rental store' is demanding that she return them and she says she doesn't know anything about no 'rental store.'"

"Jesus. What's the other call? I'm not sure I'm ready for Mrs. Armstrong."

"It's Dolores. I have no idea what she wants, but she's pissed. I wish you would tell your ex-wives to quit taking out on me whatever it is that you've done wrong. I don't have time for this, Louie."

Man, oh, man. Baja California sounded so good right then. So hot. So far away.

Did I tell you about my weakness for women with big eyes? "Put Dolores through, Evangelina. Tell Mrs. Armstrong I'll call her back. She's at a phone where I can reach her, right?"

El Corrido de Rocky Ruiz
(The Ballad of Rocky Ruiz)
—Manuel Ramos and Mercedes Hernández

> Voy a cantar un corrido
> Aunque los haga llorar
> Nunca olvidar debemos
> Al valiente Rubén Ruiz.

> Rocky, así le decían
> Fuerte como una roca
> A su gente se ofreció
> Cuando lo necesitaron.

Nació un hijo de Tejas
Joven, valiente y atrevido
Un hombre que creía en paz
Esposa e hija a su lado.

Rocky, así le decían
Fuerte como una roca
A su gente so ofreció
Cuando lo necesitaron.

En el lindo Colorado
Por su gente se peleó
Oportunidad pidió
Y por eso lo enterramos

Rocky, así le decían
Fuerte como una roca
A su gente so ofreció
Cuando lo necesitaron.

Cobardes lo emboscaron
Con mascarillas de diablo
Le acribillaron la espalda
Rocky los puños como arma

Rocky, así le decían
Fuerte como una roca
A su gente so ofreció
Cuando lo necesitaron.

Lo que él ha comenzado
Hoy hemos de acabar
Nunca olvidar, recordemos
Oportunidad pidió

Rocky, así le decían
Fuerte como una roca
A su gente so ofreció
Cuando lo necesitaron.

201

Christmastide, 1363–and, at an abbey in York, two pilgrims lie mysteriously dead of an herbal remedy. Suspicious, the Archbishop sends for Owen Archer, a Welshman with the charm of the devil, who's lost one eye to the wars in France and must make a new career as an honest spy. Now, answers as slippery as the frozen cobblestones draw Owen into a dangerous drama of old scandals and tragedies, obsession and unholy love...and murder by poison, ice, and fire.

In the bestselling tradition of Ellis Peters, THE APOTHECARY ROSE marks the arrival of a bold and quick-witted detective in this expertly detailed, engrossing tale of medieval life–and death.

The Apothecary Rose

Candace M. Robb

"Finely detailed work, authentic characters, and a credible plot...Essential for historical fans."

–*Library Journal*